Melissa Benn was born and brought up in London. She studied political history at the London School of Economics and has been a writer and journalist for over ten years. Her articles and essays have appeared in, among others, the *Guardian*, the *Independent*, the *New Statesman*, *Marxism Today* and *Ms* magazine, and in several anthologies on culture and politics.

Public Lives is her first novel.

MELISSA BENN

Public Lives

PENGUIN BOOKS

PENGUIN BOOKS

Published by the Penguin Group
Penguin Books Ltd, 27 Wrights Lane, London W8 5TZ, England
Penguin Books USA Inc., 375 Hudson Street, New York, New York 10014, USA
Penguin Books Australia Ltd, Ringwood, Victoria, Australia
Penguin Books Canada Ltd, 10 Alcorn Avenue, Toronto, Ontario, Canada M4V 3B2
Penguin Books (NZ) Ltd, 182–190 Wairau Road, Auckland 10, New Zealand

Penguin Books Ltd, Registered Offices: Harmondsworth, Middlesex, England

First published by Hamish Hamilton 1995
Published in Penguin Books 1996
1 3 5 7 9 10 8 6 4 2

Grateful acknowledgement is made to Faber and Faber Ltd for permission to quote from 'The
Love Song of J. Alfred Prufrock', from *Collected Poems, 1909–1962* by T. S. Eliot

Printed in England by Clays Ltd, St Ives plc

For Paul

OLIVER: Lindsay Fontaine? Sure I've seen her. I saw her once on TV. Lindsay's who people are. These days. That's who people are. They're like that.

David Hare, *The Absence of War*

People pay for what they do, and still more, for what they have allowed themselves to become. And they pay for it simply: by the lives they lead.

James Baldwin, *No Name in the Street*

PROLOGUE

*F*or a long time I did not know who he was, this gentle man paid homage by stern-faced politicians and academics, benign actors and acerbic novelists, quick-witted journalists and a thousand students. I watched their faces when they arrived at our parties, the specially invited; watched them watching him, greeting newcomers at the door with just a smile, taking their coats with all the good manners of a well-treated butler. Not allowing them to linger, not just then, as so many wanted to – still a little flustered by the rituals of arrival or bright-eyed from their pre-party drink. Instead, ushering them through into the low-lit living room, where my stepmother, Rachel, the party's human centrepiece, stood laughing over by the window, cigarette and glass in hand. Waving a dumbshow hello to everyone, even the bores. Only at the evening's end would one or two get their long conversation with Tom, these debates usually taking place in the brightly lit kitchen, by the fridge or next to the sink, already crammed full with remnants of the evening: paper plates and chicken legs, lipstick-stained glasses and cigarette stubs. There stood Tom and his opponent for the night, surrounded by a ring of eager, puzzled, yawning spectators urging them on to greater heights of argument, commensurate with the expected catharsis of the midnight hour.

Tom often disappointed them. He was a quiet man, thoughtful. Taking his time with words and phrases, wanting to get it exactly right.

On the phone they sometimes asked for Dr Martin or T. E. Martin, the name printed on his book covers, beneath the dust-jacket picture that I loved so much. Here, he looked brave, leonine: the close-cropped greying beard and deliberately twinkly eyes – an *effect achieved, I am told, by dabbing some Vaseline on the camera lens. The hint of the plain black polo neck. Plain T. E. Martin: the most distinguished political scientist of his generation, says his counterpart in Harvard, who comes to stay with us once a year for three weeks and orders his breakfast from Rachel as if she is running a hotel.*

This much is obvious: children rarely perceive their parents in relation to the outside world; instead, they see them on a perpetual threshold, forever promising or threatening to betray a promise. We knew who Tom was in the house, how it changed when he was working, muting us like piano music when you press the bronze pedal. We weren't afraid of him — oh, never — but we so longed to be considerate, muffling our screams when jumping from the third, fifth, seventh step of the main stairs into the hall, running up and jumping back, up and back, a continuous succession of dull thuds, so that he could write undisturbed; closeted in his top-of-the-stairs study; inking out words in that close, beautiful script of his. Using always the dark, marbled fountain pen given to him by my mother, with whom he shared an exaggerated respect for well-crafted objects.

Of his university life, we thought only in functional terms: there were papers to sort out, people to talk to, students to teach, desks to sit at and telephones to answer. As in a bad dream, each object and act had the same importance. We rang him at the university sometimes to pass on messages for Rachel. Usually Kate, my younger half-sister, would dial the number with a great show of finger power and I would hold the receiver, a newly sanctified, outsize object in my hands. When I finally spoke to him, his voice did not sound as usual: it was both indifferent and kind, calm in comparison to my sea-front shouting of instructions about fresh meat or changed appointments.

Beyond all this, I wished him only to say something simple, something that would connect up the disparate elements then pushing at me, coming up to adolescence and losing that child's myopia which is called innocence.

4

But he would say nothing, for he is thinking of rescheduled appointments and shop opening times. With the natural lack of empathy that the slow workings of time breed into those without much of it – in the present, as it were – he has no conception of my position, a half-daughter in a family otherwise complete, or of how I might imagine my half-sister and brother to be inevitably more 'placed', the word that does for love, than I was. Or how their mother, Rachel, might feel not like my own kin but rather like a good but complicated friend. And what child of eleven understands the true meaning of that ordinary, extraordinary word 'friend'?

Tom thought only that he had done his best, salvaging the product of a bad early marriage and giving it a new and happy home.

My mother – an academic, too, and now relocated to America – was never spoken of with anything but respect. Her regular letters and parcels were left gingerly on the kitchen table, as if they were bombs. And it was 'up to me', the most familiar phrase of my childhood, if I wanted to show their contents to anyone. Once or twice, the parcel contained a book of her own, which I cannot say I read except for the precious inscription. Twice a year, she would come to visit me, take me out – a daily walk on Hampstead Heath, a week in an Edinburgh hotel. Some summers, I would visit her among the skyscrapers and solid steel of a West Coast city, trail after her in the town within a town that was her campus. Here, I saw exactly what kind of life she'd made for herself: independent, respected, a little bit lonely. The danger in her life came, perhaps, from her misplaced pride. It did not come, as with Tom, from his very success, the drawing of all sorts to him, with their own motives: benign, malevolent, known and unknown.

Dissident. Activist. Agitator. These were the words of that time. They say very little, blunting true edges or blowing things up to romantic, dreamy proportions. In reality, Tom was an odd, freelance character, an intellectual who found his true talents in politics; a man who found his vocation finally and fully in protesting against the sufferings of others. Like many of his generation, he was a communist in his early youth, leaving the party over Hungary in 1956. On 21 August 1968, the day the Russians entered Prague, Kate and I ran through all the rooms in the house, shouting: the Russians have gone in, the Russians have gone in, while Rachel wept in her bed at the cruelty of invasion. But the more public side of Tom's career began with Vietnam, when he penned an 'Open Letter to the President of the United States' during the bombing of Hanoi. Need I say, this was not a 'Dear Mr President, How are you?' kind of letter but a dense working of the themes of good and evil, terror and sovereignty, power and capitalism. It was published first as an essay in a left journal, then picked up by the features editors of the national qualities. One newspaper, going through a particularly liberal phase, published the first third of the essay, which ran to 3,000 words. It caused a mild furore, and leader writers began to talk of 'T. E. Martin and his cohorts' or 'those overheated individuals of the ilk of Mr Tom Martin'. Which meant, of course, that more of his elegant, sober articles were used and more leader writers fumed about him. Then he appeared and was good on television; so that kind of fame came to him, aged forty or so, although he was never famous as politicians or pop stars are famous, only good-works famous.

We had had a quiet early sixties. Now it all changed. Tom's students – those who agreed with him – began to come to the house; the favoured for evening tutorials where the wine would be opened and the sound of argument would spiral up to the bedroom I then shared with Kate on the second floor. And the letters from strangers began coming: I saw you on such and such a programme; I read your article in such and such a publication. I feel so strongly that what is being done in America is wrong, that so much of what is being done in this world is wrong, I want to be part of the solution. I will be in London on such and such a date. Is there anything I can do? And we children would open the door to a man of six foot

6

in a trilby with a scar across his cheek to whom we would give a glass of water and a sandwich, or a young woman who had run away from home but had good shorthand. Come in, come in, we were told to tell them. Wait here in the kitchen. Here, in the living room where the sun slants on to the bare wooden floor. Someone will be here soon to talk to you.

In essence we were told: there is no such thing as a stranger.

Rachel, the warmest and yet the most suspicious of us all, used to say to us: if you want privacy, go upstairs. That's your right. The division between one kind of life and another began at the first step of the stairs leading up to the bedrooms, the step just to the left of the print of Guernica, *that long, rectangular record of suffering which hung in the front hallway.* Guernica – *rearing horses' heads and torchlit fists, swollen feet and human winds – that picture became the paradoxical but inviolable marker between worlds, ours and theirs. Beyond that step, strangers go no further.*

My schoolfriends used to say how exciting it was in our house: the cream phone jumping off its bracket in the kitchen, all those meetings in the sunny front room, the telly business. Sometimes they would send a car for Tom or the cameras would come round to us. We would peek through the double doors as men with wires as heavy as snakes moved our things about with a barely concealed disdain. Eagerly we gave them tea, biscuits, smiles. They hardly looked our way, neither the sour, kind ones who did the heavy work nor the mean smiley ones who practised their nods for the camera against the background of our clumsy clay sculptures.

But at least television and the articles meant a bit more money. Enough for proper holidays and a good washing machine. We stayed in the tall, thin house at Mornington Crescent, in the road that curves close to the railway line. Rachel got a new car, Tom a new suit. But there were to be no au pairs, no cleaners, nothing like that. Tom and Rachel were adamant that we were all to remain unspoiled, unchanged by change itself. We had to rely on ourselves, which meant Rachel really and the odd friend or student who helped out on the domestic side. Girls like Karen North, who saved our life, as we used to say. Girls like Karen North, which is where the real story begins . . .

PART ONE

1970

Some kinds of weather bring their own message. They tell you what you should or shouldn't do, exactly how to abandon old plans. Searing hot sun, for instance, scotches all but the strongest resolutions. It demands homage or a hiding from, preferably in rooms with grey slatted light and long, low couches. Serious rain tells us something similar – but only the heavy kind that imitates a hundred horses peeing or an audience near angered by its own rapture. It can tell you: wrap yourself up safe and warm behind streaked windows and drawn curtains; lie flat on your bed and make careful preparation. Or it tells you: splash out hatless, no caution required; stomp the streets like Gene Kelly, twirling with attitude.

She came on such a rainy day, some time between Christmas and Epiphany, our Christmas tree still squatting dully in the front bay window. Ten o'clock in the morning. A rap at the door, so hard I could hear it from where I was lying on my bed.

On my way downstairs, I pass Rachel on the first-floor landing, arms full of baby-soft laundry. 'I've let someone in.' She says it mysteriously.

'Who?'

No answer. She has already glided past me, into the bedroom.

Downstairs, a girl in a red wool coat with a floppy hood is waiting in the front hallway, peering at *Guernica* for something to do.

'Hello.'

'Hello.'

Her hair is sticky from the rain. She has large, pale grey eyes.

'I'm waiting for something from your daddy.'

'Oh, him.'

I say it in no particular way, but still she laughs, throwing back her head. The gesture makes all her teeth look spiky from underneath, like a wolf's. From the kitchen, I can hear Kate talking in a low monotone and Jack squealing. This means she is tickling him, probably too hard. Sometimes he can go blue in the face and you have to turn him upside-down, hit him on the back and, later, bribe him not to tell Rachel. He is her baby, after all.

'Can you spell?' the stranger asks suddenly.

'Just try me.'

She looks around for inspiration, the way people do when they play I-Spy. Turning to the picture on the wall: 'Picasso.'

'No problem.' I spell it.

'Fascism, then.' She crosses her arms across her chest.

'F-A-S-C-I-S-M . . .' Outside, the rain pounds resentfully on the street. 'Look,' I say patronizingly, 'I spelt totalitarian the other day. It's *things* I'm not so good at.'

'Right.' She nods, understanding immediately. 'Colander, razor blade, porcupine.' The words are coming faster and faster. 'Fridge freezer, aerodrome, automatic . . .'

'That's not a thing,' I protest at her last choice. 'That's a *process* . . .' There is a soft, thundery sound in the upper reaches of the house, a gathering of force. People are coming down. 'I'm Sarah, by the way. Sezz for short. So what's your name?'

We were getting near the end of the school holidays and I was used to talking this bored way to everyone. So what d'you want? Where's so and so? What's on telly? I was so bored, I'd even stopped fighting with Kate and Jack. When I saw them in the morning at breakfast, I just wanted to go back to sleep. I couldn't be bothered with Kate's tricks and Jack's jokes. Or her jokes and his tricks, for that matter. It seemed I could love them only when I didn't see them. Like last year, when I went on holiday with a schoolfriend and I was lonely the whole two weeks away. I was never happier to see my sister and brother than when they came to meet me at the railway station. They both looked so fresh and new standing on the platform in the cool morning air, watching the window of each passing carriage for a sight of my face.

But this stranger was different. She had a sharp line of energy all around her, the kind that makes you want to stand up straight, but not military straight.

'Karen,' she answers my question. 'But some people call me Kay.'

'Like the initial K?'

'Could be. But it's spelt with an "a" and a "y". Like Fay.' The wolf smile again. Everything seems to amuse her in the false way that people get amused in other people's houses, especially when they are nervous.

Rachel walks down the stairs with an empty laundry basket and a fixed, polite smile. Tom comes after her, padding soft as a leopard in a pair of two-tone airline slippers. Everybody's eyes are shining with different messages. Rachel, conveying an electric irritation at interruption, especially on laundry days; this itself part of a bigger, blunted, loving bulletin to Tom about the people he brings round and what he expects her to do about them.

Tom's signals are, as always, of preoccupation. Even on family holidays, he opens a newspaper the moment we get settled on a beach. He even tries to read a book at lunch and at dinner. We have pictures of him like that: soup spoon in one hand, book positioned away from him, near as a hand-held mirror to a vain face. At breakfast, he talks to us as if we are at a seminar. The good thing is, he doesn't notice that we don't notice.

This morning, he is holding a thick pile of printed papers in his hand. No hello from him either, but it's a friendlier silence as he offers the papers to the girl in the red coat. They both seem to understand what they are about. Now he is thanking her for doing something she is about to do. Proof-reading, correction of some sort. I can tell by the way he is talking that he is deep in a writing mood, his head still upstairs. He is down here only because Rachel has made him come down – for politeness and to save her the trouble.

My eyes are shining too. It goes with a fizzy feeling in my blood, a tightening on the surface of my skin. Tom and the Kay woman – in my head, I think of her as K; it's neater than Kay – are talking about how she could do the work here in the house, starting next week, if she wants. Oh, she wants, I can tell. Blushing red and saying yes with pretend slowness.

Rachel passes us again with the laundry basket, muttering, while I jump around saying: yes, yes, yes, start tomorrow. So what if school begins soon and I won't even be here during the day? I need entertaining now. And I know this K will be fun; not like the others who hang around in term-time or come for meetings. They are so busy trying to impress each other, and Tom especially, that they never even look at me, except to say flat thank-yous for tea and coffee.

There's a desk we can put up in the living room, I offer.

My new friend looks flattered at my attentions. Tom is laughing, his hand placed over the soft top of my head, as if I am an American football he is about to throw. Whatever his mood, he always notices us children eventually. As if we are part of some private self he cannot bear to put entirely away.

She was there the next Sunday, sitting at a specially put-up desk in the living room. This was my favourite room in the whole house. I often came in here just to sit quietly, usually on Sundays when the shutters were drawn, letting through only thin knives of light that danced with a speckled dust. I liked it best in the twilight, when the light calmed to a blood and honey glow, softening every object, faces especially. Unlike every other room in the house, this one was stuffed with things: vases, statuettes, musical instruments, books, bottles, paintings, plants, rugs, photographs. My favourite painting hung above the mantelpiece. It showed a slim, blonde cinema usherette in a long blue dress with a red stripe down the side looking sadly at the floor. I thought: she wants someone to look at her, hold her like people hold each other on the blue and white screen; with that same intensity.

We had another picture by the same painter in the upstairs hall. In this one, a middle-aged man was tending a red pump at a petrol station in the middle of nowhere. A bank of trees flamed behind him; even the cool evergreens seemed to be on fire. Looking at it, you didn't just think of the loneliness of the man in the picture but of all the loneliness in the world, as if it had been gathered up, concentrated and put on to the one canvas. Whenever I stood in front of it, I felt just as sad as the man bent by the petrol pump. And when I saw it once at a gallery, it seemed that all the strangers crowded around the picture shared something, a kind of dullness. There was nothing

15

we could do about it. We just had to keep on looking, speechless and alone.

All our best furniture was in the living room: heavy, unmodern pieces from another age. In the corner of the room was a drinks cabinet in the shape of a grand piano. There were all sorts of interesting clear bottles with foreign labels hidden beneath its lid. Mostly vodka and gin. Next to it, two old cellos propped each other up. One had its neck broken, though you'd never know from a distance. It was one of Jack's cruel jokes to offer strangers a 'go' on the cello and watch the horror on their face when they picked up the instrument and the neck came clean away in their hand. In another corner, a wooden swan the size of a domestic cat sat serenely on the rug. Rachel had carved it at art school.

My favourite item was a couch that had once belonged to Rachel's mother in Berlin and had been shipped over by her family in the early thirties. I liked to sit in the middle section of this couch, running my hand over the soft creamy material, looking into the eyes of its many colours: pink, blue, green, yellow. It spoke of infinite luxury; french windows and mornings of hope. I often lay stretched out on it, propping my head up on some cushions. From here I could study the photographs of Rachel's family – father, mother, sister, herself – set to the right of the mantelpiece. Even in black and white, you could see the shades of a dramatic colouring now inherited by Kate: black glossy hair, white skin. When any of the women of this family wore red lipstick, she looked like a star of the silent screen, geometrically cut bone and huge eyes, haunted by the shadows of history. My father's side was browner, softer, like me. The faces of his family did not leap out from their portraits in quite the same way. Patience and goodwill were required before they surrendered their story.

Now K the stranger is sitting in the room, working at a desk like a child at her homework. The shutters are wide open and all is cheerful light.

I walk over to the table and pick up a card-index box. 'What you doing?'

'Compiling a list for your daddy.'

From the scattering of white cards on the table, I can see the strange hieroglyphics of faraway places: CALIF., MASS., WASHINGTON, DC.

'Do you know a lot about foreign affairs?'

'I wouldn't put it like that, no.' She sounds a little surprised.

This was the phrase Tom had used about her that first day, when they were 'talking her over' at breakfast, the way they talk so many over, speculatively, definitively. Speaking as if he was trying to convince Rachel of the necessity of something; she, as usual, was not keen to accede. Or not immediately. Rachel prided herself on her independence and judgement, her belief that proper decisions take time. My father, impeccable and creaseless in his blue cotton shirt, spreading his toast thinly with Marmite, was speaking each word as if it did not need to be spoken, falsely casual.

The girl was keen and interested, he said, not the usual student type. She had travelled alone, in her year before university, and that took character. She had even worked in America, on Senator so-and-so's campaign – a slight nod from Rachel to indicate, yes, she understood the significance of Senator so-and-so's campaign, thank *you* very much. Tom ploughed on, showing good humour but no strategy. He should have understood: Rachel didn't want to be told the young woman was remarkable. In some vague way, that reflected badly on her.

'Well, she just wants to help,' he finished lamely. 'She thinks what we're doing is important.'

This 'we' I understood as a matter of instinct. 'We' meant more than family, more than friends, more even than the aggregate of casual visitors, the casually visited. It was a mood, a feeling shared by the special few. Like Joe, Tom's favourite student a year or two back, who still came round to see us. Joe looked like a Mexican, with blue-black hair and a smart, clipped moustache. He liked to call himself a street fighter. We saw him sometimes on television, shouting in a road full of people and rain, or sitting on a high stool, wagging his finger. But he was so kind! When he visited us, usually to harangue Tom for his conservatism with pretend fury, he brought me outrageous words to spell, written out on the back of scrap paper.

This kindness was part of 'we'. I assumed it, turned my face towards it, made my decisions by it. The older, gruffer, not-so-kind ones were sometimes on television too, sitting on tubular leather-and-chrome chairs in bare studios, attentive to each interviewer's questions, however absurd.

This, then, was the widest meaning of 'we': a language, a kind of faith. Tom was telling Rachel — and me — that the stranger spoke it, possessed it. And because I trusted him, I trusted her.

I say to her now, 'But you've been in America, haven't you?'

'If that's foreign affairs?' Her hair is different today, swept back into a ponytail. Cleaner, lighter. Today she is very grey-eyed pretty.

'I've been to America. My mum lives there.'

'Yes, I know.'

'What else do you know about me?'

'Oh, lots and lots of things.' She pretends to think for a moment. 'For instance, I know that you're not bad at spelling.'

'Not *bad*! I'm the best in my whole class.'

'Only teasing.'

I walk round to the other side of the table so that I can see her face properly. She has laid out all her pens in front of her. Each one has a different coloured ink in it: red, blue, black, green. 'You know the Statue of Liberty?'

'Yes.'

'How do people get up to that crown thingy? Do they walk or take a lift?'

'Take a lift, I guess. It's a very long way up.'

'I know a *lot* of Americans. Have you heard of Charles Reisner?'

'Of course.'

'He teaches at Harvard now. Tom says he's so clever, he's devising a whole new constitution for America! When he comes here he takes us for tea at the Ritz. The sandwiches are fantastic.'

'Lucky you.' But her voice is polite rather than warm.

'Well, only when he's here. Really not that often at all.' The last thing I want her to think me is a snob. 'Have you met my sister, Kate?'

'Not properly.'

'You might find her a bit young. She's only eight. But Jack's awfully sweet. He's obsessed with death. He thinks carrots and cabbages feel pain, just like animals. He says he can hear vegetables screaming.'

'Oh, dear.'

'Yes, he's very sensitive,' I say conversationally. 'Well, we all are – except Kate. She's a little bit more rumbustious.'

'Ah!' A patient expression keeps falling across her face. 'I'd love to talk some more, Sarah . . .'

'Oh, call me Sezz, *please*.'

'But it will have to be later.' She gestures at her index cards.

'Just guess how old *I* am . . . and then I'll go. Promise.'

'Well, actually I know that already.' The patient, amused look has gone. She hesitates, then says, 'And I know something else that will really surprise you . . .'

'What?'

'Our birthdays are on the same day.'

'No!'

'I only just found out. Looking through some files and things . . .'

For a moment, I am simply shocked – 'No! Not the very same day?' – then I am ecstatic at the news. It confirms the special friendship I felt for her from the first moment.

'Oh, can we do something? Together? Can we do something? Say yes. Please, say yes . . . And wait until I tell Rachel. She just won't *believe* it.'

Karen North is not the first person to make the move from hallway to kitchen, not the first stranger to knock on the front door and be welcomed in as 'family'. But no one else has done it in quite the same way, offering not friendship but availability, not merely her self but endless small acts of service. Those others need prove nothing to belong. Goodness is not their game. Like Rachel and her friends, closeted in the kitchen, where they smoke, talk and laugh for hours with that insistence bordering on malice I will for ever after associate with women in my mind. This is my stepmother's other life, reminding her of an existence before marriage and children, foreshadowing a possible life after it.

By contrast, Tom's friendships come to life in the more muted world of the front living room. Mostly they are men, like the lively Joe or Lou, a news journalist. Lou loves a good-tempered quarrel, even with us kids. Especially with us kids. What, he asks Kate and me, do we think of drugs or underage sex or soul music? Kate always has an answer ready. What's more, her tone delights him. Myself, I find Lou's bearded face a little intolerant, his speech too much like gunfire. On the few times I have tried to answer his questions myself, his impatience freezes me into near silence.

Outside the closed door, we hear only low-volume, confident talk; an occasional crescendo of rehearsed anger. Kate and I are sent in with trays of tea and sandwiches and everyone makes a great fuss of our fuss. A shy, spotty young man in the corner, one of Tom's students, nervously takes down what everyone is saying. His fingers are splodged with black ink; he has screeds of paper on his green-trousered lap and a crease of worry across his oily forehead. I give him more cake than the others, while Kate entertains the main group with tales of violent goings-on in her London primary-school playground.

I am continually astonished at and jealous of my sister's ability to embellish a perfectly ordinary story with such style. I have often witnessed the same incidents that she describes; they never looked like that to me. More than that, she can seem to wheedle some general point out of her tale – exactly what my father's friends want.

Back with our empty trays in the kitchen, we continue to eavesdrop. We even peer through the inch-wide crack in the folding doors that mark the boundary between kitchen and living room. The talk is an odd mix of the high-minded and base gossip. Peace, hunger, gender, race, justice, right, wrong, left and right: all these terms make us yawn. But the stories about x, y and z and who is sleeping with whom are just riveting. Lou is the best source of these stories. He is always commenting on people and their shady pasts, their sordid secrets. There's so-and-so who is not to be trusted (read: spy). And so-and-so on his paper who is going through a mid-life crisis. He left his family for a young female photographer who looks just like his wife (Don't they always? Rachel says later).

Then there is talk of Tom or possibly Lou or even Joe putting themselves up at the election, which is expected soon. An 'Independent Justice' candidate, to run against the official party. 'We've got to pick a good old right-wing Labour bastard,' Lou says joyfully. 'Someone with a bad record on the war, the unions, race.' 'We could run the campaign from here,' offers Tom. 'I've an old Gestetner in the loft. There are always people to help. Even the kids could do something.'

'Just like all those years ago when they used to send children down the mines,' Kate whispers to me. But I know she is pleased, as I am. For the simple reason that things will continue to *happen*. There is nothing more exciting than a season of political activity. Our regular bedtimes will be disrupted. Strangers will always be profusely thanking us for doing things our parents don't even notice we are doing. And the phone will ring before breakfast, after midnight, its insistent bell, the most thrilling sound in the world.

Karen sits with the men in the living room sometimes. Always on the same patch of floor, between the drinks cabinet and the sculpted swan. Here, she does not wear her hair tied back in her 'practical ponytail' but freshly washed and hanging loose. A frosted pink lipstick puffs up her lips and makes her look like a secretary. There is a studied, almost mournful look about her. On the rare occasions when she does speak, her voice is low with nerves and she scrubs furiously at the square inch of carpet in front of her.

Everyone says she is full of ideas. Lou and Joe adore her, which is something to do with sex, even I can see that. When four students are shot down at an American university for protesting against the Vietnam war, it is Karen who comes up with the idea of a special public meeting, Karen who suggests flying over some famous Black Panther man from the states. Great idea, Lou says, sitting on the edge of his chair, eyes half-closing with political pleasure.

Outside in the hall, when the meeting is breaking up, Karen's face is pink with pride. Lou congratulates her again and Tom gives her two phone numbers to call from our house. When the others have disappeared and it's only us juniors left – Kate and me, Karen and Joe – she and Joe practise kung fu in the hallway. High kicks from the hip and lots of chopping motions with their hands. Karen tackles Joe to the ground and starts to throttle him, legs astride his solid trunk of a body, while we clap them on from our ringside seat on the stairs.

With us as a family, she is practical, earthy, forever mending. Ground-floor things need fixing; she fixes them: drains, fuses, squeaky hinges, the fridge light, the front-door bell, wobbly shelves and picture frames. Every time we pass *Guernica* in the front hall, she stops and looks at it with a frown. 'There's something not right about that picture, Sezz,' she announces eventually. 'We're going to rehang it, you and me.' Sure enough, the heavy black frame is laid face-down on the kitchen table while she attends to it, picture hooks between gritted teeth, steel wire looped round her strong, thin fingers. 'Doesn't take a minute to hammer in new hooks on the wall,' she says in a strangled voice.

I hold the picture steady while she pushes it about, a tilt up, a tilt down. (At our feet, the blue gas light of the hall heaters splutters gently, graciously.) 'Stand back and let's see,' she says after a while. However, the hallway is not quite wide enough to give us the perfect balance. In the manner of a moral, she tells me, 'Good as it can be. You have to say that. The best I could do. Now leave it.'

In the evening, after the younger ones have gone to bed, we sit on the couch in the living room. Sometimes we watch television. Or we talk. Karen gives me sips of beer. She is teaching me how to inhale smoke properly, blow it out through my nose in two parallel paths, like a storybook dragon. And she tells me about sex and love things, in a stern, instructive voice. My favourite story is about how she lost her virginity, or was 'deflowered' as some girls at school coyly call it. I've heard it four or five times now and never tire of the story. He was a photographer she met at a party when she was sixteen. He took her to a huge studio with a four-poster bed and there made love to her twice, without a word spoken. The next morning when she woke up, he was gone.

She never saw him again.

It is this part I can never get over, his apparent cruelty. We return to that question more often than the technical matters of torn skin, blood on the sheets and funny feelings between your legs, fascinating as all these are. Karen seems unbothered.

'He was ever so good-looking.' She takes a drag on her cigarette, then passes it on to me.

'And do you have a boyfriend now?'

'No. Not exactly.'

'But you wear that sometimes?' I point to an amethyst ring on the fourth finger of her right hand, her only piece of jewellery. 'When I first saw it, I thought you were engaged.'

'Engaged is left hand, silly!'

'Oh. It's a lovely ring, though,' I say wistfully.

'Thanks,' she says, getting up from the couch to go through to the kitchen. The wooden doors have been folded back and I can see her from where I'm sitting on the flowered couch. She moves quite differently in our house when Tom and Rachel are not here – tonight, they are at the cinema – as if it is her house, her fridge, her bread.

'I'm going to make a sandwich. Want one?'

'No, thanks.'

'You can do me a favour, you know, Sezz.' She is speaking with her head half inside the fridge.

'What's that?'

'You know I've never been up those stairs. Ever.'

'What stairs? Where?'

'Here. I mean here. I've never seen the rooms upstairs.' Her head pops questioningly round the side of the fridge door.

'So let's go now.'

'Now?'

'Now.' I want nothing more than to please her.

We walk slowly up the stairs, careful as burglars, nervous of Kate's famed wakefulness. Since I have moved to my own room on the top floor, she and Jack share a room on the first floor, next to Tom and Rachel's bedroom. I can hear the quickening of Karen's breath, the fear in it. On the first landing, three blank doors face us, enclose us, like changing-room mirrors. The main bedroom door is to the far left.

Quickly I push it open, resisting the rusty moan of unoiled hinges.

Strange to enter such a familiar room with an outsider.

The room looks like a museum or a scene from a dream. Each element, from the pattern on the carpet to the ordered pile of books at the bedside, takes on a new, mysterious meaning as I see it through Karen's eyes. The solid tomb of a bed with its dark coverlet, lit by a pile of white pillows at its head, is the centrepiece. Little surrounds it: the flat, ungiving surfaces of cupboard doors, closed drawers. A table at the window where Rachel does her night-time studying, is piled high with shiny textbooks. A swirl of women's clothing – something long in a light silk, something chunky in darker jersey – hangs over the back of the desk chair: clothes discarded this evening when she was choosing what to wear.

And standing at the window, overseeing the street, the judgemental figure of a shop dummy, a chalk-white mannequin blithely wearing a skewed pile of Rachel's hats on its head, scarves and bracelets wound around both its sharp, bent arms.

I walk over to the dummy and steal away the topmost hat, a black pillbox with a short lacy veil, and drop it on my head. 'What do you think?'

Karen doesn't turn round. Standing by the mantelpiece, she is staring at a row of family photographs. Plain family snaps, in colour. A portrait of Jack, aged five, all freckles and ears. Kate and I, astride the back of the couch, giving false bright smiles. Tom and Rachel's wedding photo. A radiant couple caught in an amber-lit interior. Rachel in long, flowing white; Tom with a smart carnation buttonhole. Behind them, peeping out from the forest of adult knees, the tiny crowned bridesmaid of the first marriage.

'That's me!'

'Beautiful dress.'

She asks me to pick up a silver-framed photograph on Tom's side of the bed, a head-and-shoulders shot of Rachel in the black pillbox hat. Eyes peeled upwards, the curved smile of a clown.

'It doesn't quite look like her, does it?'

'Probably because she's younger.'

'No. I mean, she looks different,' Karen says. 'Like a different person.'

'Tom says that's his favourite picture. She was wearing that hat when he met her. He says that whenever he's cross with her, he only has to look at that to remember why he married her.'

'Is he angry with her often?'

'Oh, yeah. The normal stuff. Stamping and shouting.'

The sweep of a headlight on the street. Karen flinches.

She wants to see Tom's study on the top floor, next to my bedroom. This room is all wood and paper with hundreds of books in ceiling-to-floor shelving. Tom's desk, an inheritance from his father, is as broad as a small boat and a gleaming chestnut brown. Sometimes I am allowed to sit with him when he's working, on the other side of the desk, squeezed up against the bookshelves because the room is so tiny. When I turn, I can run my finger along the edges of all the spines. My favourite books are his, four slim volumes kept in the far right-hand corner of one set of shelves.

'Look!' I say, proudly picking up a hardback published in 1968. His *Collected Essays*. What a clever man! To be collected by people! Read by people! And still to be himself, his kind, blurred face now looking back at me from the book jacket.

Karen is peering from the tiny picture window that looks out to the garden. A huge, undisciplined may tree reaches nearly up to here. In daytime, its thick branches cut out the possibility of a clear view across the backs of the nearby houses and gardens.

'Did you know,' she said, 'it's bad luck to bring sprigs of that stuff indoors?'

'I took some to my teacher last year when I went up to secondary. And *she's* still alive.'

'Might have had bad luck since. You never know.'

'Her boyfriend did leave her actually. She was sobbing in the corridor after classes. I saw her.'

This is really one of Kate's school stories. But if she can retail some of my observed experience, why can't I do the same with hers?

'Ah-hah, then. So your may sprigs did their job!'

Karen is now sitting in the big swivel chair, lightly touching each of the handles of the desk drawers, trying one for fun. It pulls open, making a terrible rattle. Fifty identical ballpoint pens. She slams the drawer shut, then pulls out the top piece of paper in the red plastic in-tray on the desk top. University letter heading. The one beneath is from the BBC.

'Better not,' I warn.

'No. You're right.' She teases the paper back into place.

'And the filing cabinet,' she says, in a voice that suggests: well, that concludes matters. 'He's very tidy, your daddy. Very ordered indeed.' She tries another drawer. Empty. 'Do you think he's happy?'

'Course he is. Why shouldn't he be?'

'Those arguments you talked about. Him and Rachel. Other women? What do you think?' She looks mischievously at me as if we are co-conspirators. Then her expression shifts to one of grave respect, as if my point of view is the most valuable in the world.

'No idea.'

'Oooh, go on, tell. I can just tell you know more than you're letting on.'

'I don't know anything.' My voice is squeaky.

But Karen seems not to notice. 'How boring you are, Sezz,' she says, in one of her nicest tones of voice.

'I don't like it at all.' Rachel's voice, irritable and amused. They do not see me, behind the bedroom door, a spot on the first-floor landing where, if I stand in a certain way, I can hear and not be heard.

'I feel as if I'm in some bad film. Every time I come home she's cleared out another damn cupboard.'

'You must find some way to tell her.'

'Tell her what? Please don't cook, clean, babysit without prompting? The girl is so available, it frightens me. You know she washed out all the cupboards in the living room and polished the silver, what little we've got?'

'The fact remains, it's your house.'

'No, Tom, it's your house.'

'Whatever . . .'

I imagine Tom closing his eyes, refusing the rise. Also, to consider the matter. Quietly.

'Sezzie's completely gone on her, hangs on her every word.'

'If it wasn't her it would be someone else. It would be your sister and she'd be drinking double gins.'

'Instead, she's smoking.'

'Not really smoking?' Worry in his voice, a trace of admiration.

'Smelt it on her breath the other day. And don't malign Penny. You always make her sound like a drunk.'

'It could be someone at school – the smoking, I mean. It could be just herself.'

'Can no fact I state stand as indisputable? It's your

house and your daughter is taking cigarettes from students' – she paused – 'housesitters, whatever they are, whatever we call them.'

One of them shifts their body weight in the bed; turns away or towards the other.

'Piety,' Rachel says in a pillow-muffled voice. 'There's a piety about her. And an odd sort of authoritarianism.'

'Now, come on.' He is trying to humour her.

'No, I mean it, Tom. Why should the young be any different? Be exempted from the niggly traits that mark the rest of us?' She says the word 'trait' as if it's something you carry things on. 'Innocence has gone by her age. At twenty-one, or whatever she is, you're a fully formed human being. At Sezzie's age, no. But college age? I certainly was.'

'Teaching as many as I do, I'm not so sure.'

Her silence is sceptical, nothing else. He continues, undeterred: 'What makes you and me better, no, not better . . . what makes you and me human beings in the better sense of the word is all the mistakes we've made. Knowledge we've profited from . . . Bad things. Good things. That nebulous quality . . . self-knowledge. That's what mitigates the piety, the authoritarianism or whatever.'

'But the kernel is there.' Rachel's voice is clear again, as if she is now sitting upright. 'Go back to any school reunion and that's exactly what's so depressing. It's not just that the little redhead who cheated in tests has that same look in her eyes and you know she's cheating on some poor husband now. It's me too. I'm the same when I look in the mirror of the school toilets, where I've run to escape the whole lot of them.' I can hear Tom chuckle. 'It's the same old weak, petty, fearful, sparky Rachel looking back at me. All I've done is learned to cover up. To some degree.'

'Regression.' He says it in his 'teaching' voice.

'Partly. Yes. But not just.'

'You're saying there's some unchanging core to people?'

'Maybe it's only goodness that grows.'

'Oh, oh, oh,' he says, tenderly, in response to her little-girl-lost tone. The sound of a soft kiss on the hard flesh of forehead. A few moments' silence, during which I want to both run and stay, curious and repelled by what the quiet means. Then, to my relief, the sound of 'ordinary' noise, noise I can set my clock by. Throat-clearing, rustling, the hollow-floored tones of getting up, of self-organization.

I drop my alibis in the hall laundry basket, pick a high-toed, innocent way down to the kitchen.

Saturday, a spring afternoon so pure you'd never believe in winters past, winters to come. Rachel takes the younger ones to Camden market and Tom goes into the university. I am now old enough to be left alone in the house for a few hours during the day, even though I usually waste the privilege by restlessly roaming the three floors, wondering where to settle.

Ten minutes after Tom has left, the bell rings. I know who it will be.

'Hi, kid.' A pat on the head.

'Hi.'

She doesn't ask if I am alone; she knows that I am. She doesn't ask if I want her to come in; she knows that I do.

In the kitchen, she begins to make tea. It's the only part of Karen that's like her mother, she says, the part that won't drink anything but proper tea. It's not simply a matter of leaves rather than teabags. It's a whole process, starting with the delicate flower-patterned teacups (mugs are 'anathema' to her, she insists), the matching milk jug, a bobbly tea-cosy and a strainer resting on its own

33

flowered dish. Karen has slowly introduced a number of items to our kitchen, given as presents to each of us in turn. Rachel received the largest present, a swollen-bellied green teapot. On occasions like this she uses them with all the pride of a well-paid housekeeper: cleaning, wiping, polishing up, setting down.

She wants to say something to me, something big. I can tell by the steady blinking of her eyelashes, her silence.

'Rachel's shoebag.' She blurts the words out, reddening slightly as she takes two sips of still-boiling tea from her cup.

'What about it?' Everyone knows that Rachel keeps a red velvet shoebag at the back of her wardrobe. It's a running family joke that it can never be opened, not even in the event of her death.

'Well, *Kate* said . . .'

More of Kate's stories, I think wearily. I know this one well. Ever since a girl at school found out that she had a baby brother born to her mother at seventeen and given away at birth, Kate has insisted that Rachel has some similar trauma in her past and that the 'adoption certificate' is deposited at the bottom of the red velvet shoebag. She tells the story when she is bored, curling her hair around her little finger. It has acquired new twists and turns over the months, as boredom piles on boredom and Jack has become more entranced by it. He has always wanted an older brother. He has also always wanted to live on a farm. Now this older mythical sibling does just that, in Sussex, Kate grandly insists, just as he does all the other things that Jack would love to do: eat porridge for breakfast, drive a pony trap, feed the pigs and walk around in a ribbed smock with straw coming out the corner of his mouth. Jack even draws cartoons depicting this brother's life.

'You mean that old adoption story?' I say cynically. Most of all I am annoyed that Kate has been talking to Karen without my knowing about it. Karen is *my* friend.

'Seh-hezz,' she wheedles, putting her hand over mine. 'I know it's probably completely daft. But just a little look.' Her flesh is surprisingly cool. 'I'll give you this for it.'

She is loosening the amethyst ring on her finger, wriggling it over hard knuckle and slim finger to place it, a challenge, on the table.

The truth is, there is no secret. Not like that. I know what's in the shoebag. Dozens of letters from Tom to Rachel, when they were first 'in love' and she was a girl not much older than Karen is now.

Sometimes, when Rachel is in a specially good or specially bad mood, she pours all the letters out on to her bed like Father Christmas with a pile of presents, swirls them about and then lies, propped up on her elbows, reading. Her expressions change from one moment to the next; a grunt here, a giggle there, a long, light sigh after that.

I toy with telling Karen all this, but think better of it. She will only ask more, ask more of *me*. We'd do better to stick with the adoption-certificate story.

'And you'll give me that −' I look down at the ring − 'in return for what?' I can't meet her eyes directly.

'Just a little look. If you bring it down here.'

'I cannot possibly do *that*.' My voice is loud, too loud.

'No, of course not.' She looks almost ashamed of her own suggestion.

'I mean, Rachel could be back at any minute,' I say in a milder voice.

'Mmmm,' she says thoughtfully. 'On the other hand,

you could go and look upstairs while I stand guard down here . . . Oh, go on, Sezz. What's the point of life if you can't be a little bit curious about other people?'

As I am walking up the stairs, taking two at a time, I am formulating a plan. It is as follows: I will go into the bedroom, walk to the cupboard, put my hand in and pick up the shoebag. Shake it, once, twice, three times. Maybe even open it, so I can tell Karen I have opened it in all honesty, but *keep my eyes shut* as I do it, so as not to see anything. No need to mention that. As I can't go downstairs immediately, I will open the wardrobe door and compose my face in the shaving mirror – *I'm so sorry, Karen. I couldn't find a thing. I didn't expect . . .*

In the event, I am upstairs for longer than I expect to be. I get drawn into my current favourite fantasy, in which I am told that the entire family has been killed in a car crash coming back from a weekend away. (Fortunately, my mother has simultaneously died in a pile-up on a Californian highway, which takes care of that angle.) Over and over again, I am walking, erect and alone behind the coffins into the church. Or I am sitting, head bowed, in the front pew. I can hear the whispers of admiration and sympathy rustling up behind me like a hundred crisp packets. Never have I loved my family so much as now, each placed before me, in their separate wooden boxes. Never have they seemed so kind, so unusual, so full of life, so irreplaceable as in this small country church.

Coming downstairs, I must still look upset because her first words are, 'It doesn't matter.'

'Nothing there,' I say a little too adamantly.

'Really. It doesn't.'

'It's just boring letters.'

'From whom to whom?'

'Oh, all about the early years, my mother and so on,' I say vaguely.

'So Kate was making it all up?'

'You shouldn't listen to her,' I say reprovingly.

For a few moments, Karen looks chastened. She is wondering if I will tell on her. Something in my expression lets her know that I won't. There is the ring to stop me. The ring, sitting separate from us both, a small chunk of solid colour. It is lucky she took it off before I went upstairs.

It won't fit me, but I still want it. A piece of Karen. To take out and consider; to put away, somewhere safe.

When she gets up to refill the kettle, I close my hand over it.

'So, tell me about your momma.'

'What about my "momma"?'

Karen and I are cleaning the floor of the living room, sliding back and forth over the smooth wood surface, our stockinged feet tucked and tied into old, torn pillowcases. On the turntable, my favourite record plays. Chris Montez singing 'The More I See You, the More I Want You'.

'What happened, that's what? Between her and Tom.'

'Well, they just fell out of love . . .'

'Just like that?' She snaps her fingers. 'No warning?'

'*I* don't know. I don't know everything, you know.'

'But why did you stay with him? Why didn't you go with her?'

We have shifted all the movable pieces out of the room: the cellos, the swan, the drinks cabinet. Chairs, lamps, tables are piled in the hallway and kitchen, the carpet is rolled up like a pancake. Only the giant couch cannot be shifted. It has been turned on its side, pushed face against the wall, draped in grubby sheets.

'She wanted to start all over again. She didn't think she could do that with me.'

Next time Karen glides past me she pats me on the head. I duck her compassion.

'Do you see her much?'

'About twice a year. Can I put that record on again?'

'Sure. So what's it like?'

'What's what like?'

'When she comes to visit.'

The record has a sugar-pink heart. Plop! It drops on the turntable. Karen is now dusting objects on the mantelpiece with a section of feather boa tied to a broken-off broom handle.

I scrabble for some order of words and hear myself saying, 'Oh, OK. You know, we get by.' But the pictures in my head are more complicated. Vivid, easily called up, I prefer to store them away like a favourite photo album stuffed under the bed with the dust balls. *That's why I jumped when you came to the door, the first day. It could have been her. The same brisk knocking. Rat-a-tat. Like a policeman. Or bad news. Rachel usually answers it and the two women embrace. How are you? How are you? I can tell they like each other; there is warmth there. Neither has what the other wants any more. Just as I know when they are talking about me, a bit later on, when I'm sent out on some stupid pretext – Sezzie, run up and get Eve that drawing, that book, that coat – their voices slur yet become more urgent, more significant. They want to say to each other: oh, Sezzie's doing just fine, really well, loads of friends. Quite settled. And then when I come back in the room, I look for the first real time into my mother's face. And I am sorry for her, sorry for how glad she is that I am happy without her; sorry for her sitting on a stranger's couch with that eager leaning-forward, knees-pressed-together look. But I am glad she chooses briskness rather than sentimentality as her response to me. This marks her out as a fine, restrained person, such as I hope to be one day. Right or wrong, it is her belief that she long ago forfeited the right to hold me, hug me, spoil me. Instead she chooses distance tempered with an enormous, hidden kindness.*

'She's a linguistic philosopher,' I say, as if that explains everything. 'Can I put that record on again?'

'Oh, not again.'

'Once, just . . . please?'

'Then that's it.'

Plop! The thin, high tune of the opening bars wraps around me one more time, drawing me to an exhilarating place I am learning how to inhabit, bury down in. 'We go to the park sometimes,' I say dreamily. 'She likes the parks in England. She says they're safer here than in America.'

Karen's smile tells me she is thinking of something or someone else, the feather boa still a stiff prop in her hand; the absurdity of her pose reflecting some absurdity of my own. There is a new look of curiosity on her face.

'What?'

'It's nothing.'

'Nothing's nothing.'

'I was thinking, you're not like a little girl at all. You're nothing like I remember myself at your age.'

I know when I am being praised. All the skin around my mouth feels tight from trying not to smile.

'And that's good.' She says it so quietly, I can hardly hear her; her first hint of low self-esteem, of some sadness in her past. We know nothing about her really. We have never asked.

'Well, don't forget what's coming up!'

'What?'

I am talking about our shared birthday, our same-day celebration: a party already planned to the last detail in my head, a party with cake and candles and invited friends, a party I imagine to be suffused with dim light and shadows, like an Old Master painting, a party where I will reign supreme, at the centre of more than affectionate attention – princess of the household for the day, with Karen as my consort, surrogate partner, best friend.

'Birthday girls,' she repeats without much interest, turning her attention now to some streaky marks on the french windows, rubbing violently on the glass with an old cloth.

Not for the first – or the last – time, my carefully laid plans are swept aside by external events. A week before the dreamed-of party, a general election is announced. The sombre newsreader enjoys making it sound like war – the end of something, the beginning of something else.

Upstairs I can hear Kate's exclamation of pleasure, then the sound of her galloping down the stairs – to stand, a minute later, before me, her whole being alight with the disorder of it.

'What are you *crying* for? We're going canvassing . . .'

She is right. The living-room group had long ago decided that as soon as the election was announced Tom would put his name forward as an 'Independent Justice' candidate – there was no alternative to this ambiguous title – in a constituency in the north-east of London. His principal objective is to sabotage the official Labour candidate, an old docker with a bad record on the war in Vietnam and immigration, a man unimaginatively loyal to the government in all its worst aspects. 'Old Dick' is a self-serving party hack, Tom says. He is not even loyal to his own kind, by which Tom means the white working class. When a local packing factory came out on strike in the late winter of '69, he refused to visit, let alone support them. He is even against the Open University, the old philistine!

All is in hand by the time I get home from school that day, the living room already rearranged, furniture pushed

41

back, an odd jumble of desks and tables lined up in a row, facing a large school blackboard that now blocks the closed partition door with the kitchen. Even as I am letting myself in the front door, some of Tom's students are hauling chairs down the stairs under Karen's direction. And she herself is radiating a new authority. It is in her voice, the lightness of her step.

She gives me a brief smile: more than recognition, less than conspiracy. At a lunchtime meeting, she has been appointed Campaign Manager. I am pleased she finally has an official function in our house.

For the next three weeks, we live and work to a rigid pattern. Karen is given her own key. Each morning she lets herself in soon after seven thirty. We can hear her moving quietly around the kitchen, making her first cup of tea, pulling a plate down from the crowded shelves of crockery. Most mornings I join her. We sit and talk at the kitchen table, eating piles of buttered toast. Soon after eight, she goes into the living room and begins chalking up lists on the big blackboard there. Plans for the day. These mark out all the people, places, meetings that require Tom's attendance, from first thing in the morning to last thing at night.

While Karen assumes Tom's enthusiasm to be equal to her own, we know better. Tom is merely doing as he is told. From greeting the local TV news reporters who come to the house to quiz him on his candidacy to the small Friday night meetings at outlying church halls, all is done from duty not pleasure. The family viewpoint is clear: *this* sort of public life – American glad-handing, diplomatic pleasantries, being nice to everyone without discrimination – is not his.

Tom is weak at the very point that Karen is strong, on the practical, the people side. In our view, it is his integrity, his finer mind, that make him so, the same qualities that lead him to prefer the quiet of his study to the raucous noise of parties, even his own. We do not suspect him of ordinary snobbery, not that. In theory, Tom appreciates every human being. In practice, most of them bore him. As it bores him to repeat the core messages of the campaign. Tom likes to speak at length, one to one. Booming through a megaphone from a moving car reduces him to the banal. I have seen him do it a few times, on Saturday and Sunday mornings in the crowded high street. He is hopeless. Everything comes out fuzzy. He emphasizes the wrong words in the wrong way. Even Old Dick can stoke up more verbal fire from a moving vehicle.

I feel sorry for Tom during the daily 'briefing sessions'. The night-time ones are the worst. Everyone has been drinking beer. They all talk at once. About what Tom should be doing. He should be saying more about the government's failure on this policy and that policy. Fact, fact, fact, fact. Karen has them all to hand: percentage-point rises and falls on prices and income, unemployment, literacy and immigration; statements made by this minister and that minister contradicting statements made by some other minister. And then there is his *approach*. 'You must appeal to ordinary people,' Karen opens fire. 'I'm thinking of people like my mother. They're the ones you should be persuading. The ordinary woman who's on her way to the shops who wouldn't vote Tory but can't put her finger on what's wrong with the government either. Who thinks Harold Wilson is simply a jolly nice man because he smokes a pipe and his wife's not too good-looking.' Tom's nose wrinkles up in distaste. 'You've got to do those people's thinking for them.' Karen finishes off with a manly swig from a beer can.

Lou isn't so interested in Karen's mother. He and Joe

are always hammering at Tom to sound less like a university professor, tenured for life, and more like an angry street fighter, more like them. Over and over again, Joe shouts out his version of the facts – 'People are *dying* in Vietnam, blacks are *under siege* in this country, in the States. It's no good analysing it *ad nauseam* like an Oxford don. You have to rouse them – make them see that it matters.'

From the doorway, Rachel sighs, so quietly only I can hear her.

It was my shameful secret, those long hot afternoons of freak good weather, how much I hated canvassing. The very activity that Kate had longed for, for which she now jumped out of bed each morning in eager anticipation of beginning, I loathed. Each time a fresh pile of leaflets was slammed on the table or shoved into my hands at a street's end, I was mired in depression. It was not just the unexpected poverty of the back streets or the loneliness of the old in apple-green hallways, or even my fear of random black dogs. It was the impossibility of comprehending so much life crammed into such a small space. For years afterwards, I could not bear the sight of long roads, each house with its own neat gate and well-tended front garden, its tidy dustbin-settled doorway.

I loved nothing as much as a door that never opened, the residents on holiday or scrabbling from an upstairs window, waving me only too willingly away. I did not have the politician's ability or instinct to imagine a common interest between all these people. For me, there was no pretending a belief in the mass of humanity. Instead, I saw the opposite: people's very difference from one another. Even in my short visits, I could spot the seething antagonisms and subtle distinctions of position

44

that marked out one from the other and were relinquished only in the face of a common enemy.

On a more fundamental level, it seemed impolite to ring people's bells at around six at night. This was just the time when we, at home, liked to be left alone and Rachel was loudly wishing stragglers out of our house. The awareness of intrusion made me apologetic, almost craven – sorry, my every second word. Young men in particular embarrassed me. I always blushed and stuttered out my standard opening: Hello, I'm delivering these on behalf of Tom Martin. Have a leaflet . . . please. Staring down at the green sheet as I passed it over, Tom's image imprinted on every flimsy copy. His face possessed none of the mournful wisdom of his book jackets. Instead, he looked ghostly, spineless.

'Independent Justice. What's that then?' It's the older ones, the men usually, who like to quarrel, even with a little girl. Rachel has told us we need not speak if we don't want to. But three gardens down, I can see Kate's sleek black head nodding up and down in involved chat. It goads me to try, at least a few words . . . 'They think there's a lot wrong with both the parties . . . but they're *not* Tories!' Cabbage smells assail me. 'If you're not Tories then why don't you vote Labour? Doesn't this Martin bloke remember the '45 government, what Labour did then? What's the point of stirring up unnecessary trouble?'

I open my mouth. No sound comes out. Perhaps he's right. 'How old are you anyway? Sending out a kid at this time of the evening. It's bloody disgraceful!'

'Well, thanks for your time.'

'Send this Martin bloke round to me.' He taps the leaflet in his hand. 'I'll tell him why I'm not voting for him!'

Later in the safety of our kitchen I will say – *and then he slammed the door in my face! I could have been badly injured!* A small lie, this. Unimportant. For the door is rarely slammed. Mostly, it's a firm click. Or I delay the final parting, embarking on a more general conversation, feeling I must offer something in return for their trouble. We chat about the neighbours or the weather in the street. I am told long stories about the people on the right who keep their dog in all day and don't feed him properly, or the mum with two kids over there who can't keep them under control, or the dustmen who leave bins just standing in the middle of the street.

Yes, I nod sagely. Terrible, I quite agree. And I do agree. I just can't think what to say or do that would help them be happier.

O n the night of the count, we stand in a huddle before
the stage, wearing our loud buttons and red-striped
scarves. Kate and I are allowed a beer. It makes my face
go red and convinces me of how much I have enjoyed the
campaign really. When the returning officer steps forward
to make the announcement, Rachel's sigh is this time one
of release. Joe, who is standing next to her, hugs with her
such lightness that, all of a sudden, I see that it's her he
loves, not Karen, and that Rachel knows it only too well.

Tom has polled a respectable 3,000 votes. Old Dick is
home safe and dry, now making his speech, while Tom
stands with his hands behind his back, mouthing his
prepared statement.

Just in front of us, Lou is shaking a bottle of champagne
like a victorious racing driver.

'Get that Martin bloke off the stage quick as you can,'
shouts one of his friends, a news photographer. 'I want to
catch him raising a glass to parliamentary democracy or
revolution or whatever other daft thing he believes in!'

Half an hour later, Tom still hasn't come into the body
of the hall to join us. All around us, people with different
coloured badges and scarves are partying.

'Where the hell is he?' Lou says to Rachel, the usual
impatient expression on his face.

'There,' she says quietly, pointing to the back of the
stage.

Tom is talking to Karen, who is gripping a clipboard
like a hot-water bottle. I hadn't noticed she was gone.

47

Now they are found, I am suddenly anxious at the fact of their previously unrealized joint absence. The way they are talking bothers me, their blindness to the outside world. Smiles in the wrong places. The way Karen is standing is all wrong, too. Her right foot curling round the back of her left leg like a bashful schoolgirl.

Tom smiles, rubbing his beard. I have never disliked him before but I dislike him now, simply and quickly, as a brush of paint across a white page. As you would a stranger, without thinking. Because he is *pretending*. Pretending to be all the things he really is: good and kind and generous and clever.

'Come on!' Lou's friend the photographer shouts at them. Beckoning them, this way.

Seeing us all down below, they wave. Simultaneously, like film stars arriving at a première. *Not bad, eh?* Karen, in particular, is elated.

Some of our group wave back. Not Rachel; she is giggling with Joe. Not me; I simply stare. Deliberately cold and hostile.

In those few moments, I know what my face looks like. I know because I had seen just that face in a family photograph, taken one Christmas Eve just after my mother had left the house, to go back to her hotel. We were sitting down to the evening meal and I was bad-tempered without knowing why. All I knew was that I didn't want to have to keep choosing. I wanted to be like Kate and Jack, part of something without thinking.

On the inside my envy spun, dark and heavy, coagulated like tar. On the outside, it looked merely sly: a young girl frowning, with mean, narrowed eyes. The way someone looks after they have stolen something from a friend and jut out their chin as if to say, why shouldn't I? Life's not fair to me either, you know.

There are early signs for the sharp-eyed. For the rest of the summer term, Tom spends almost every evening at college. When he is at home, he sullenly retreats to the top study. Rachel spends too many Sundays in her dressing gown, trailing through the downstairs rooms. On warm evenings, she calls me out to join her on the back step. She wants someone to sit with her while she drinks beer and files her nails, our talk following the slow, deliberate rhythm of her emery board, back and forth, back and forth, lazily repeating itself over territory of no apparent consequence.

When the holidays begin, Karen takes me over to the Heath to swim. Two bus rides, changing at Chalk Farm. Our favourite pitch is a slope of grass that leads down to the ladies' pond. One blazing hot day, we lie in our swimming costumes on a scratchy check blanket that makes me itch. Karen's heart isn't in it. I can see this in the way she sprawls beside me. Her body is spread-eagled like the dead in detective films and she is roused as reluctantly as a teenager. 'What?' she accuses me, when I touch her lightly on the shoulder. 'What do you want?' She has glimpsed a new world and the old will no longer do. She wants more now than to belong to our house, to our family, more than to be loved by us. We have shrunk finally to human size.

Suddenly, she sits up, raising a hand to shade her eyes. 'What should I do, Sezz? You're good at schemes and things. I need to get away.'

'Then get away,' I say sadly.

'No, really. Everyone needs something new sometimes.'

'A holiday seems the logical thing. Or maybe a boyfriend.'

I want her to laugh like she used to.

'Oh, God, Sezz-pot. You'll be suggesting I take up stamp-collecting next.' She leans over and ruffles my hair. 'And you? What about you?'

'What *about* me?'

'I lost the plot somewhere along the line. You've changed.' She is catching words from the air, not paying proper attention – at first. 'Yes,' she says after a second, pushing her sunglasses over her head. 'You are different. Maybe it's you who's got a boyfriend all of a sudden. Come on, tell.'

'There is absolutely nothing to tell,' I say stiffly. 'Except of course that I turned twelve a few weeks ago.'

'Oh, shit!' she exclaims. 'We forgot all about that, didn't we? The party and everything.'

'I didn't,' I say sullenly, looking down to the pond. A last few swimmers are splashing in the green water, their happy calls threatening to turn sad at any minute.

'Birthdays don't mean so much when you get to my age. I still have your present, though. All wrapped up, under my bed.'

She says it so lightly, so naturally, I am sure she is lying. 'Tomorrow. We'll do swaps tomorrow. You *have* got me something, haven't you?'

'Of course.'

'I knew so.' She rolls back on her tummy.

'So come for lunch.'

'*Very* grown up now. "Come for lunch," says the queen of her castle!' Her voice is muffled.

'One o'clock.'

'Precisely.'

I knew, I think, that she would not come. As I am buttering the bread for the sandwiches, thick yellow butter scattered with salt; as I am grappling with the tin opener for the can of salmon; as I am slicing the cucumber paper-thin. As I sit alone and waiting behind my pile of sandwiches on the kitchen table, spread before me like religious offerings on an altar. It's over. Don't ask me how I know. It's just this: I can no longer *see* Karen, sitting opposite me at the kitchen table as she has done so many times before. I try to imagine it and the chair is empty. The house is empty. Of her.

The final detail is inconsequential: a telephone message left the next day — something about a cheap flight to America; a small piece of white paper neatly folded in two like a clue in a treasure hunt, left on the table in the front hallway. For me to stumble upon. As if by chance.

When the 'troubles' come in the early autumn, we children are told nothing. Even the bedroom door is firmly closed to eavesdroppers. All I can see are shadows. All I ever hear is the word *something*. *Something* to do with the university. *Something* to do with a charge brought against Tom. *Something* to do with a young woman called Barbara. It is frightening that we have never heard of this Barbara or seen her in all our lives.

Who is she?

The house is quiet, the steady drip of visitors firmly turned off. A few steadfast friends still come round, but they visit as people do after death, bringing gifts to ward off evil spirits or their own pity. Lou never comes without a whisky bottle and Joe rings twice a day, too anxious for ordinary greetings, wanting to speak to Rachel straight away.

When we talk at night, Kate and I swear that we will never forget their loyalty. This, we say earnestly, is what really counts, not all the political stuff, not all the partying. As we talk, we become more extreme, exhaust ourselves with our determination to sift out the moral lessons from our fear. We hate the partygoers now. We remember them with resentment. Small things they once did that made us laugh now provide clues to their bad character that we guessed at all along. The reverse applies to our true friends. *Their* loyalty was obvious from the beginning. Look at Joe – *he* never ignored Rachel, as so many of Tom's political friends do. Lou's very rudeness. He can cut through to what really counts. We love their refusal to take any of these events personally, their glib assertions that it is all political, a way of getting at Tom.

In the kitchen, Rachel rehearses elements of the *something* with Tom. These days, he carries a pile of papers thick as a family-sized cereal packet around with him. He is always consulting so-and-so's statement, his own 'depositions'. But his continual shuffling angers Rachel. 'Stop *looking*! Just speak. From the heart.' Her next sentence confuses us still further. 'Remember. Lofty detachment. That's your tone. This-is-of-course-nothing-to-do-with-me-but-I'm-participating-in-deference-to-the-surreal-fantasies-that-you-people-have-constructed.'

Kate and I, sitting, knees drawn up on the big couch in our nighties, give each other sidelong looks of fear, amazement.

You wait, she says, my comforter. *You wait, it will be just as it was*.

Then comes the morning that Tom leaves for the meeting that will 'resolve his future'. I am allowed to straighten his tie, its boldly floral pattern looking like bad judgement in the bright sunshine. Kate brushes imaginary dandruff from his dark-suited shoulders. Jack reties his shoelaces, crouched at the shiny round toes like a chimneysweep humbled before the master's fireplace.

You wait. Kate says it again, while we are waving from the living-room window.

No, I think. It will never be the same. I know that now. There may be the same conversations, the same actions, the same people – and they do flood back in the weeks after, brimming with relief – but the change is made. I can see it in their eyes. Even after we are told that Tom has been cleared, that the *something* has evaporated, that we are safe again. Rachel glitters with a new determination and my daddy is wild and lost around the eyes, even as he drinks champagne from one of Karen's teacups in the kitchen.

The words used: exoneration, vindication, complete, total, absolute.

The telephone bell rings all day. Whoops of jubilation.

Joe brings a Stollen cake stuffed with marzipan; Lou, his usual whisky.

Never the same. I see that. Tom is relieved but his quietness is a different quietness now. Not self-sufficient quietness but pain and tooth-trouble quietness; night-time and unpaid bill quietness. It is as if he has moved a half-mile away from us all and he is never going to come back. Ever.

The empty champagne bottle, the hollow cardboard cover of the Stollen cake, are still propped up against the kitchen dustbin when the card arrives. Postmarked New York, early August. At first I think it is from my mother, until I recognize the familiar, loose handwriting.

Its only message, the words: AT LAST THE ORIGINAL! Unsigned.

Turning it over, I stare at a grim reproduction of *Guernica*. All that evil and suffering on a card only six by four inches.

'This was sent nearly six weeks ago. She must be back by now,' I say to Rachel. 'She'll be round soon, when she hears.'

'Don't count on it,' says my stepmother, turning her back on me as she reaches in to get something from the fridge.

Karen North never visits our house again.

PART TWO
Karen

Who was Karen North?

That question, when asked later in her career, could be answered most easily by the facts. She was born in 1948 – the same year as the National Health Service, she liked to tell journalists, with mild irony – the eldest child of divorced parents. One sibling, a brother, two years younger, Alan North – later something respectable in the City. It was, she always insisted, 'a very ordinary kind of childhood'. No highs, no lows, no *drama*. To her more intimate acquaintances, she gave the tale a slightly different emphasis, the accent being on her desire, formed early on, to escape. She told them of lying in bed, aged thirteen, looking at a large may tree outside her bedroom window and dreaming of the moment she would climb out of the window, shin down the tree's bark and run away to the nearest big city. 'Which is exactly what I did – metaphorically speaking.'

There was no may tree; she borrowed that imagery from Tom Martin's study window. But the feeling about herself all those years ago, that was true enough. She had always wanted to run away from home, from the small country town where she was born, a town replicated a thousand times the length and breadth of post-war Britain. It was in the south-east, but it could have been anywhere; a town with a mass of squirrel-grey and brown houses huddling off the main road, a town with a thin strip of shops – the post office, the ironmongers, the sweetshop

57

selling dusty lemon sherbets in giant glass jars – leading down to the railway station.

Standing at the sweetshop door, you were diagonally opposite the church, with its neat graveyard, its well-clipped hedges and a short stretch of pebble-dash wall where the teenagers sat on sultry summer evenings, passing the crazy orange tip of a cigarette between them.

To most of her neighbours, the church constituted the symbolic centre of town. They were respectful if not deferential towards the largeness of the geographical and moral space that it occupied. The church held Karen's attention for a quite different reason: it was from its furthest north-eastern corner that the sea road – such a romantic name for a wide strip of pot-holed grey – began. Leading at first past the respectable, rose-pretty cottages belonging to the town's middle class and the holiday visitors, coming after a quarter of a mile to the high walls of the doctor's house, where on summer evenings you could hear the hollow cork-poppings of tennis games, smell the perfume of comparative wealth. From this point onwards, it was not much more than a path, travelling through wild hedgerows, then taking a sudden sharp bend left, after which you could see the sea, steel grey, beyond a marshy field. Hop over a rusty gate and it was only ten minutes' uneven walk to the sea wall.

In her early teenage years, Karen would often tramp the sea road, wondering whether to follow it on for the few miles further that would take her to the town where her father now lived. He had left when she was eight years old, her brother six; a note propped tidily on the hall table. Upstairs, two freshly dry-cleaned suits, still hanging in the bedroom cupboard.

Karen tried to imagine it sometimes – swinging her giant black wellington boots on the sea wall, staring at the red buoys bobbing helplessly in the winter sea – her mother smiling and strong. Strong enough to leave and be left, a hundred times over. The convincing image never endured: the soft mist over those pretty, helpless blue eyes returned. And the silence of the pine and tidy hallway continued to resound. Any noise, however harsh, however startling – a ringing telephone, a whistling kettle, a voice laughing in the sitting room – was always swamped by the inner voice of their house; the voice that is created and sustained in every dwelling by the unspoken thoughts and feelings of its occupants; the voice that every visitor hears, willingly or not, the moment they walk through the front door.

It was this simple desire – *not to be my mother* – that led Karen to create her own story, her own mythology, a mythology of difference and strength. In the tale that she constructed for herself, there were significant moments in her progress; such as the day when she was twelve years old and her brother quick-swung a golf-club behind him and hit her full in the eye. At the first moment of impact, she was convinced of immediate blindness – a small voice emerged out of the darkness she was holding in the palm of her hand; speaking to her of sad, thin reconciliation. But the bone had protected her, as the doctor from the high-walled house later assured her. The golf-club had clean missed the eye and she was left with only a few stitches that healed to a pale drawing of past suffering. When she opened her eyes in the doctor's white-walled consulting room, overlooking the tennis courts, and saw her mother clear before her, muttering predictably and paradoxically about both miracles and small mercies, she knew that she was saved for some purpose.

Tall, strong Karen. Saved for some purpose. From adolescence on, she had an appealing plainness of manner.

People looked in her almost pretty face and were warmed; 'direct' and 'straightforward' were the descriptions that came most easily to them. She knew that she was liked, knew that she would always be included, if only because people were afraid to leave her out. Observation of others less fortunate showed her these were not gifts to be spurned. Instead, she must make the most of them, help them to bring her what she needed – escape, and a chance to play on a bigger stage.

For this reason, she was especially polite to her form teacher, who knew about university placings, and a neighbour who read *The Times* from cover to cover, and a friend of her mother's who had once lived with a cookery journalist in London and had written a small volume of poetry. In each of these people, she saw a potentially useful section of the unseen whole.

If, at school, she pretended to be lazier than she was, this was purely to deflect hostility and the petty oppositions of jealousy. She made friends in the playground, especially with the tougher girls, who then beckoned her on to the church wall on passing Saturday nights. There were boyfriends who initiated her into the casual pleasures of sex: snogging in the back of vans, underneath tables at parties. It was she who always wanted to go further; they who pulled back, a little alarmed at her confidence, her enthusiasm. She shrugged her shoulders at their timidity. This alarmed them even more, the bald fact that she cared no more about their refusal than their acceptance.

She was fourteen when she first found her father's house, walking the sea road on impulse one schoolday morning. It was at the far end of this seaside town – she could hear the soft rush of the waves coming up the pebble beach as she tried to find her way down the main street – beyond the elegant bell tower, beyond the town's one Chinese restaurant, in the section where the quiet people lived. She had found his address in the phone book, just like anyone else, followed the tributaries of an old map with her forefinger until she'd come to the right place.

It was larger than she'd expected, more sure of itself, a corner house, freshly painted white. There was a glass porch and yellow roses that appeared to be scrambling wild up the outer walls; only on closer inspection could she see where they'd been pinned at regular intervals.

It was past eleven when she reached there. A frosted window on the first floor was raised a few inches. Karen could sense, rather than see or hear, someone moving beyond it, in the cool interior. It wasn't her father. No man could glide that way, take possession of a room without audible sound. It was his woman, *my stepmother*. A slight, subtler presence.

Karen took a step back and then another. Without thinking, she turned round and began to wander the neighbouring streets until the town clock struck eleven thirty. A schoolgirl with books and a windcheater attracts no attention on a late morning in a place like this. Returning, she saw the window was eased shut. Silence had settled around the house like deep snow.

Just one look, she told herself, advancing up the garden path. (Neatly laid flagstones, the curved black lines of earth shorn of the unnecessary, the straggling weed.) Just one sight of her father's life through the glass door; his old outdoor coat in brushed dark grey wool, or his briefcase, or a pair of his shoes. Of all his things, this was what she missed most, his lovely, heavy men's shoes, brown brogues punctured with holes as definite as a teenager's bad skin or the shiny patent black leather of Saturday evenings out, dancing.

Now, through the clear glass, she could see a narrow

hallway with coat rails, bags and the expected shoes. But these were not a grown man's shoes. Or an adult woman's. What she saw first of all was a tiny pair of shiny red wellington boots, the cheerful gleam of their surface matched and reflected in a perky red plastic hat, hanging on one of the hall coat pegs. Next to them, a pair of blue leather sandals, a delicate fleur-de-lys pattern sculpted from the soft leather of each toe. Silver buckles polished bright as a coffee-spoon.

From where she was standing, she could even see into their soft beige interiors, see a black number '6' stamped at the same spot deep within each foot.

It did not occur to her to question whose shoes these were. There was no pretending; why should there be? They belonged to a little half-sister about whom no one had told her and probably never would. (Perhaps her mother did not know, even now?) From the size of the shoes, Karen guessed that the child's age was approximately four, maybe five. It did not bother her, this small addition to her life. It interested her.

She stayed outside the house until the town clock struck twelve. Her instinct told her that the stepmother would be home soon, for lunch, busy with a basket piled high with wrapped vegetables. Before leaving, she circled once more around the house. There was a huge picture window at the back, looking over a beautifully laid-out garden, but the curtains were drawn and she wouldn't climb over the side gate. She returned to the front, wanting a last look at the little girl's shoes.

It was the sandals that affected her the most. The way that they stood, neat and uncomplaining, waiting only to be found a use. Although they were party shoes, they looked as if they had less fun than the other things, the red boots, the rain hat. And for that she felt sad.

*

At seventeen, she worked hard for her exams, studying late into the night in her bedroom, copying learned lines on to fresh white cards she had bought in her father's town. This was what she did every Saturday morning, walk the three miles there and back. For stationery, she insisted to her mother: the pens and paper were so much better in the big stationers on the parade where cars parked at a crazy angle, their bumpers nearly nosing into the glass frontages of the shops. Hoping to get a glimpse of her other family, especially her baby sister. She did not see them once in the main street but the notebooks and the index cards were lovely all the same, etched with thin blue lines as watery as human veins. On each card she wrote her major headings: 'The Revolutions of 1789/ 1830/1848', 'The Paris Commune', 'The Dreyfus Affair'. Karen was good at history, English, politics. All the subjects that required a sensible absorption of fact and a laying out of argument in competent fashion. She was an excellent school debater.

On the day of the exams, she arrived later than her schoolmates, leaning on a glass door away from those who were happy to talk about how nervous they were. The usual questions bouncing back and forth: *Did you get your revision done? How much? How much? Do you think that question will come up?* She merely shrugs, *Enough. Enough.* A cigarette was defiantly poking out of her shirt pocket. *As soon as I'm finished, I'm out of here.* In the exam hall, the expected nausea of the first few moments. She had words for that, too, a whole unbreakable code; words to spur herself on, words to congratulate or comfort herself. By seventeen she had created her own moral world.

On the day when the envelope containing the exam results arrived, she drove – her mother's car; permission not granted – to the beach in her father's town. She sat at a spot hidden beneath the sea wall, the cold pebbles giving way with a rush. Setting the envelope down next to her like a cherished companion, she piled stone upon stone on top of it, until only the edges of the white rectangle were peeking out from underneath their weight; stones sticky with traces of green weed and salt. Before her, the sea was slow rolling in.

Behind her, a narrow boardwalk, the occasional tread of a passer-by. Wednesday afternoon: the town was busy with itself indoors, unknowingly individual. It changed on the weekends. Then the boardwalk was squashed solid, families mostly, idling along from the pub to the eel van, from the fish and chip shop to the small converted terraced house that sold ersatz Cornish cream teas. The other concession to the tourist interest was a shop selling thick cable-knit jumpers in cream or navy wool. People dawdled in front of its window, straightening a jacket or a stray curl in the half-hearted reflection. On regatta day, all the disconnected colour from the town was sprayed across the sea, a hundred jolly stamps speeding and still in the far between.

Dream-staring one minute, then brutally pulling the peek of white from underneath its intolerable weight, tearing open the envelope. Two As and a B. Even she, sitting cold and alone on a deserted beach, was flushed at the success of it.

Karen did not reach London, her ultimate destination, for two more Septembers. It was true what she told Tom Martin about her year off travelling to America and France and Germany. She had even spent a few days in the campaign office of a left-leaning Democrat senator in New York, stuffing envelopes and answering the phone, experience later lovingly elaborated on her CV as early 'political campaigning'. Returning to England, she made straight for the northern city where she had elected to study political science, the university picked on the advice of her knowledgeable form teacher. Here she was unhappy, the six months later remembered mainly as a freeze-frame picture of herself in pyjamas, with a can of beer in her hand, hanging on the battered old pay phone in the corridors of the halls of residence, ringing home; her mother's habitual loneliness a grotesque, distorted confirmation of her own. It did not take her long to understand the feeling for what it was: the gift of warning. The next day, she marched to the appropriate office, singing loud and clear the message: let me transfer to another place, another city. Get me to London. Get me out of here.

It was strange how one man led her to another, a chain of covert involvement in which she pulled the strings. (Or so she thought.) For a long time she believed the first one was the least important; a plump, attractive young man who lived on the same landing at the halls of residence, in an anonymous grey building a few minutes' walk from Warren Street tube. His name was Michael and she had picked him out during the first week of term, determined not to make the mistake of her wasted year at the other place, the mistake of isolation. What drew her to him was his mouth, a female film star's mouth on a bull's head, piercing dark eyes and a high colour that suggested excitability.

He was delighted to be stopped in the dim-lit corridor and asked about street names and course content and then, more immediately, the paperback peeking out of the top of his duffel-coat pocket.

'Ah, George Orwell!' she said knowingly, when he fished the book out and dangled it before her.

'Like him?'

'So-so . . .'

'You might prefer this.' And from the other pocket, he pulled out a book by E. M. Forster: *Howard's End*.

'Take it,' he said, when she hesitated. 'I know where to find you if I want it back.' He nodded towards her numbered door.

That night she sat up in bed, drinking warm beer and

eating take-away pizza. Apart from every Agatha Christie ever written, she had never read a novel before. It took her till four o'clock to finish this strange tale of two highly strung sisters and a silly house in the country.

'Snobs,' she said to Michael the next morning, catching him as he came back with a copy of *The Times* tucked under his arm.

'Who?'

'The Schlegel girls.'

'Read it already?' He allowed himself to look impressed, before hurrying on to benignly correct her. She was wrong, of course. It was not the Schlegels but the Wilcox family one should berate, for their slavish devotion to trade and commerce, the so-called real world. How shallow could you get, with this devotion to property, this ignorant refusal to see that the real world was in the spirit?

Over breakfast in his room, calming down after the consumption of four bagels in a row, he explained that the Schlegels were based on two famous sisters, one a writer, one a painter, who had lived not far from where they were now. Fitzroy Square was about three minutes' walk away. 'I shall go and have a look,' Karen said dutifully, mostly because she wanted his friendship.

The next day she walked down to the square. It had an appealing bare aspect. Black wrought-iron benches were placed every twenty feet round its perimeter. She chose a bench at random and sat down. It was one of those perfect autumn days when each colour is a preternaturally clear representation of itself; as if the azure blue of the sky or the bloody rust of the chimney stacks had been separated, distilled and then painted back on to the picture of the day. She had never cared for weather at home, it cut her off from something essential. Here, in the city, it seemed to bring things together, harmonized the parts of a whole.

So this is one piece of what I am, after all. She picked out a house to stare at. With the book and its resentments so fresh in her mind, she could almost see the shadow of the Schlegels flitting in their absolute certainty from floor to floor. What a high-pitched life to have, then and now! But only if you were one of them. She didn't know whether she loved or feared them. She remembered what they were like to Bast, apparently kind yet freezing him out with their devastating politeness. He could not break with their power. He broke under it, eventually.

Unlike Michael, it was the solid Wilcox family who repelled her least. She felt she understood them, what they wanted; nothing too grand or ethereal, only to work, acquire wealth and property, to succeed in the most conventional of senses. To possess the outward signs of success and respectability, reward for their hard work, no cant attached. Whereas the Schlegel sisters did not even know what they had. She saw women like that at college already; pretty and confident but strung high on pure feeling, as if their brand of undiluted sensitivity was a virtue in itself. Underneath, they were greedy for the continuation of a success they had never earned in their own right.

That people should want power and success was obvious to her. She did not make a philosophy out of it; it would take years for her to understand the place of instinct, her own included, in political viewpoints. However, she also wanted to fit in, and the age was idealistic. It found its purest representation in young men like Michael who lacked the courage to accept the luck they'd been born with.

In him, she witnessed the fruitless struggle of someone

who could not embrace the obvious. His father was a solidly successful businessman and upright citizen, generous giver to charity and local JP. It was obvious that his first-born child deeply resented the twenty-five years and £25,000 that his parent had over him. He could not wish to emulate it. Nor could he let it go! Even as he asked Karen to come with him to look 'at a tiny scrap of a flat' his father was going to rent for him at the back of Farringdon.

'Should you be taking the place if you dislike him so?' she asked, straight-faced, as they stepped out from the halls of residence.

'I don't see why not,' Michael said, with a hint of irritation he was trying to turn into joviality. 'Might as well squeeze the old bugger for all he's worth.'

It was worth something, this 'scrap of a flat', the first floor of a doll's-sized house set at the top of a gently sloping hill behind Farringdon. Even the name of the road, Back Hill, had a romantic, otherworldly ring to it. There was one main room and a small kitchen, and a tiny toilet hardly big enough to squeeze into. When Karen went for a pee, her knees nearly met the door she was trying to pull shut.

The front windows overlooked the dull metal of the doors of a warehouse opposite. As dusk crept on, the light and sound were magical. There was none of the remoteness that characterized their poky rooms back at the halls of residence, suspended too high above the street, above life itself. Here, this empty space soaked up everything that surrounded it; the calling of the men out in the street as they manoeuvred their lorries out of the tight, cobbled street was as close and real as the words she and Michael spoke inside the room.

They sat cross-legged on the thick red carpet. Behind

them, the creamy walls caught the dipping of the day's light, the flickering shadows of passers-by, puppet men in huge square-shouldered jackets carrying giant oblong bags.

She looked across at Michael fondly. He was good-looking, earnest, not much more than a boy. She could not take him seriously, partly because he treated himself with such extraordinary gravity. The way he talked demanded a listening at a double level: there was a difference between what was said and what he wished to say; anger disguised as altruism; ignorance disguised as tigerish opinion; common prejudice disguised as high politics. His best words were reserved for writers – George Orwell, E. M. Forster, Henry James, Jane Austen, George Eliot. Light and loving, creative about the uses of language itself, he became heavy, unoriginal when he talked about the world: *the need to get involved with events beyond one's immediate experience, the importance of becoming part of change.* He was not political, or not in her terms. He lacked the necessary hardness, the empiricism. He had the temperament of an essayist or one of life's perpetual students. He would never be able to stock an office or order an army out.

At eight o'clock, when the room was so dark that she could barely make out the features on his face, Michael suddenly stood up and she thought, wryly: he's going to kiss me. At last, the proper use of that extraordinary mouth.

'Shall we go?'

She admired his ability to avoid the obvious when it came to sex. It made her more willing, eager now to follow him in their quiet walk down narrow streets strewn with cardboard boxes and rolling bottles. The London they saw here was poorer: abandoned market streets bordered on one side with high walls; on the other, sudden grim openings to vast, shadowy housing estates. They came upon a cloistered wealthy square just as unexpectedly. Here, even the mailbox was draped with rich green ferns.

At nine o'clock exactly – she heard the chime of bells from a faraway church – they crossed the threshold of a pub, uncarpeted and empty except for a few old men at the bar and a couple of teenagers playing darts. A pint of Guinness quickly drained, quickly replaced. Euphoria building and banking in their eyes; Karen saying less and less, Michael more and more; both in expectation of the same event.

Now Michael was talking about a lecturer at college who had inspired him to *look at himself, to get involved*, a man called Tom Martin. Superlatives were tumbling out of his mouth, curling up the corners of her cynical heart. The most brilliant academic, published three books by the time he was thirty, once a typical liberal who had been changed by speaking out against the war in Vietnam, supporting moves for student democracy at the college. There was nothing obvious about him, Michael insisted. Such a careful man.

'Careful?' she interrupted. 'That's an odd phrase.'

'Strategic,' said Michael triumphantly, wiping a cream moustache from his top lip. 'I mean, this man is no fool. This man is *clever*.'

'Yes, I got that.'

'No, but you *haven't* got it,' Michael said patiently. 'I can tell by your face that you think he's just anyone, and I can't persuade you otherwise. You must see him for yourself.'

'OK,' Karen assented, stubbing out a cigarette in such a way as to mean, show me to him some time.

'And he's got a really gorgeous wife who's much younger than him,' Michael said gloomily.

'Don't tell me, she's a professor of advanced biochemistry and their children are mathematical prodigies?' She didn't mean to sound this sarcastic.

'What *are* you babbling on about?' Michael said innocently.

'I just hate too-good-to-be-trues, that's all.'

'Ah, but some people are just more . . .' But his tongue had thickened and the right word didn't emerge.

'I'm terribly hungry,' Karen said brutally.

Michael reddened at her rudeness. 'I'm sorry. I'm forgetting my manners. I've some basic stuff in my room if you'd like to come back and eat with me. Cheese, tuna, bread, olives.'

Already, her mouth was watering. There was nothing in her small fridge but two cans of beer.

'Are we far from home?' They had walked to so many places, she had no idea where they were.

'No. We've come almost full circle.' He was touched by her use of the word 'home'.

'Good,' she said almost sleepily, draining her glass and wondering if he made love as he talked, with such dogged commitment, in such utter good faith.

From the moment she saw Tom Martin, she understood.

She would have called it love at first sight, if she were more innocent; if she hadn't been with men already and knew herself with them, the sensations they could evoke in her – the heat travelling light and insinuating as a spider along her arms, legs, up the back of her neck; the tightness in her abdomen, between her thighs. That these sensations came from Karen's body and not from the heart – in her view, the refuge of the romantic schoolgirl – did not mean there were not dimensions beyond the body involved; moral, even political ones. She would not have been attracted to the man if he was there to discuss refuse collection or biochemistry. She would not have seen beauty in his height, his gravity, the simplicity of what he wore and how he wore it. (She was not above admiring a man who knew how to dress.)

No, it was precisely her knowledge of his connection to the world, and a world beyond the dry one of books and ideas, that filled out her image of him as he stood, waiting, on the stage below. Her knowledge that gave greater play, more dimensions to his simplest gestures: the idle rearranging of a few pages of yellow lined paper on the lectern, the pushing of a pair of horn-rimmed spectacles back to the bridge of his nose, a half-smile directed at a girl with long blonde hair in the first row. Observing it, Karen felt a stab of jealousy as painful as heartburn.

His lecture was one of a series on 'World Politics: 1945

73

to the Present Day', a bland title tailored to fit the requirements of an exam syllabus. The fact that the hall was full and buzzing with a curious excitement before Tom Martin even spoke was testament to his acknowledged skills as a teacher and a speaker. People came to hear him not just because he ranged further and wider than most of the lecturers, not just because he was an acknowledged star of the university, but because they genuinely wanted to see what it looked like, how it moved . . . *political commitment*.

He did not disappoint her when he began to speak – a beautifully orchestrated story of the Cold War, the struggle of two continents, two traditions, each with impure souls, each with its strengths and weaknesses mirroring the other in faith and tyranny. He spoke not just of governments and leaders, but of buildings, books, paintings, national character; Eisenhower, McCarthy, Kennedy, the Bay of Pigs, the Rosenbergs. He said: I want you to step back, I want you to understand America before you condemn it or emulate it. He said: we cannot know it if we do not understand the quality of light in the glass tunnels above Grand Central Station or the dreams of Jay Gatsby, the luminosity of Marilyn Monroe or the cut-glass perceptions of Henry James. *Each artist uses a different language but we can comprehend the same idiom at work* . . .

It didn't matter that she listened so hard mainly because she wanted to sleep with him. She was learning something, as much about style as about content. Let others scribble like obedient animals, Michael next to her, noisily scratching with his pen, cheeks apple red with excitement, the blonde girl in the first row, occasionally tucking a sheaf of hair behind her ears in mock industry. In some glimmering part of her Karen saw that the words spoken would not translate on to the lined page of an exercise book. *Never*

74

*forget how evil manifests itself, the simplicity of it and the
obviousness. Its banality. Never forget, too, to look beneath, rise
above the obvious. That would be my best advice to you at twenty,
or even forty. Never accept the facts at face value.* She would not
accept the facts at face value – surely, if she stayed
completely still, he would eventually notice her among the
herd of 200? Surely, in the next fifteen, ten, five minutes
remaining, *she* would get her half-smile?

And then suddenly it was over. No warning; the students for the next lecture already pressing at the doors,
restless, teasing their predecessors for their absorption.
Fifty minutes, over. All around them, young women were
stooping like Degas dancers to pick up bags from the
dusty floor. Tom Martin was talking to the girl with the
long blonde hair who had climbed on to the stage. Karen
felt a stupid desperation at the thought that she would
never see him again.

She didn't know if it was good or bad luck, but the girl
with the long blonde hair was sitting at their table in the
bar afterwards. It seemed Michael knew her. Her name
was Barbara and she was as pretty close up as Karen had
feared. Her friend Sheila had a soft, round face and
brown frizzy hair; Karen found it easier to address most
of her remarks to her. Five minutes later, an older man
joined them. He seemed to know the Barbara woman,
who squeezed along the leather seat to make room for
him. Harry somebody. His last name sounded like 'Bells',
but it couldn't be. The noise around them was deafening.

The others were still talking about Martin and the
lecture. Praising, offering insignificant criticism, praising
again. Michael was all puffed up like a producer or an
agent: this was my man, I led you to him . . . so there!
Perhaps it was the girls – not quite the Schlegels, less

75

questioning certainly but prettier, the blonder one at least
– who brought out the perverse reaction in Karen. Perhaps
it was the strength of her own feeling about Martin and
his powers – for secretly she, too, agreed that he was
'charismatic' – but Karen could not join in their routine
approval. She had to distinguish herself from the herd by
picking a small quarrel with one or two of Martin's
propositions about America. Ready, if any of them came
back at her, to invoke the easy phrase, I should know,
I've been there.

No one came back at her in the event. The two girls
looked curiously at her as she spoke; when she finished,
the round, brown one shrugged and Barbara shook her
silky hair and said, 'Well, he's *my* tutor and he lends me
his books from his own shelves', in a so-there tone of voice.
Michael merely looked embarrassed, as if Karen had
burped in public.

Only the older man seemed to be on her side, although
he said very little. She felt that he was watching them all
with his deep-set blue eyes, but her especially. His face
looked familiar in the way that the faces of people we are
instantly drawn to sometimes do. A crew cut, an unfashion-
ably solid leather jacket.

When he was getting a round in, she asked Michael
what his name was. 'Harry Wells. He's a mature student.
Weird bloke, if you ask me,' he said stiffly, still annoyed
with her for her criticism of Martin.

'Sorry.' She stuffed a hand in his pocket, as lovers do. 'I
did like him. I liked him enough to want to try and get on
his course.'

'Really?' Michael looked sceptical.

'Really.'

Harry Wells came back from the bar and put the drinks
down on the table. Wine for the girls. Bitter for Michael.

For her, a pint of lager. 'I did say only a half.' She smiled, nodding outwards, as if to indicate that the noise was to blame.

'Thought you deserved more,' he answered, holding her gaze for a second longer than was necessary.

So he was her third man, the most crucial of all, the one who offered her a part in Tom Martin's life far more significant than she could ever have hoped for. It didn't take her long to figure it out. Harry Wells was part of the same pattern, part of her fate; that was the silly girl's word for it, wasn't it? The word that someone like Barbara would have used, after consulting her stars in the evening paper?

It was as if he were conducting a courtship, the way he approached her indirectly, surrounded her, moved in on her. Whenever she went to the photocopier or to buy a sandwich in the canteen, he would be standing by the counter with his own sheaf of papers, his own tea, his own intent. She would get in a lift and there he would be, pushing the same floor number as her own. Walking along an empty corridor towards her and then changing direction, so that he could walk the rest of the way with her.

You could always see him coming. Short hair, trousers with a knife-edge crease, the ice-blue eyes. Edging forty, his skin was like a baby's. He was a mature student, he told her, one of the few who actually wanted to learn. They both smiled slightly, in mutual understanding. During one conversation, he made a passing reference to 'rich kids like Michael Bannister who think they want to fix the world to rights when it's themselves that need fixing'. Ah! She'd found a soul-mate at last!

Harry Wells was solicitous of her progress. How was she

getting on with her attempts to switch on to Tom Martin's option? He was the first person she met, standing in the hallway outside the administrator's office, when she learned that she'd succeeded.

'Let me take you for a drink,' he insisted. 'To celebrate.'

Was it then that he made the first suggestion? His first allusion to a possible job in which she might be interested? It was so subtly done, she might not even have noticed in the high flush of excitement about her transfer. Or was it the next time, when they were having one of their habitual ironic conversations about lefties, women's libbers and the double standards of the rich?

That phrase, she always remembered the doubleness of it. 'You could help me out – and yourself, too, if you want.'

The fact was, she could not remember the precise moment when he made his suggestion and she assented to it. It just all seemed to fit. It was about a month after she had switched options. That was late November, around the time she had handed Tom Martin her first essay – on the achievements and failures of the Attlee government – and was nervously waiting for his response. Around the time that she overheard Tom's secretary, Hilary Churchill, say she was looking for someone with proofreading skills who could double-check the manuscript of Dr Martin's new book.

Karen lied about her previous experience to Miss Churchill and the manuscript was hers. She didn't dare tell Michael what she'd done; Harry helped her out here, too. He brought her a book of proof markings and tested her over two days until she was as skilful and confident with a soft blue pencil as a professional.

They were in it together, then. It took nothing to slip into the next stage, to hear Harry saying: *You could do even more. It's so easy to do, get into his house, a dozen or more of the chosen ones flock there. And on weekday nights!* And to smile at his promise that she, too, could become part of the family. How did he know that this would be her weak spot? He simply did. Spotting a hungry, wistful expression on her face . . . 'You're curious, aren't you?'

'Yes, just to see,' she said weakly.

'See how different it is, you mean? From the rest of us ordinary mortals?'

It wasn't as crude as that. It was more than curiosity, less than need, but not that much less. As if an arrow had begun to move and she was connected to it; not to follow it, not to go with the gathering force, would be to go against nature itself, to drop into a void as vast and meaningless as space. Now that she was so near to Martin; he had smiled at her during a lecture the other day and she, to her amused shame, had flushed a quick, fluid pink from forehead to chest, sweat rising in the bony cavity between her small breasts. A few minutes later, she had dabbed the spot surreptitiously with a forefinger, sampling her own passion and embarrassment.

She had to know how a man who talked like Tom Martin on stage lived on the ordinary scale. Hard to imagine him yawning, or rinsing out cups of coffee at the sink, or taking toilet paper from its crinkly outer skin of wrapper, throwing out the old, useless cardboard tube, slipping the new roll on to the thin black rod at the back of the door.

And she wanted to see the perfect beautiful wife, the child prodigies, the thin, narrow house full of talk. Happiness: she simply had to see how it was done.

Neither she nor he ever used the absurd self-dramatizing words that described her intelligence-gathering: spy or its clumsier counterpart, informer.

Yet that is exactly what she was, what she became.

They met every second week in the darkness of a Russian tearoom in Soho. Sometimes, waiting for him, she looked round her at the dark wooden tables squeezed tight together and the hunched shoulders of conferral and whispered to herself, yes; just the single word yes, over and over. Once again, she was excited by the sheer physicality of the city, from the hard reflecting silver of the spit-clean teaspoon now held in her hand to the distorting glass of buildings, the biscuit stone of pavements, the deep cobalt blue of the tube signs, the silver lining of lifts. How different from the water colours of home and its antiseptic suffering. Everything happened here: sighing love affairs and big break-ups, meaningful arguments on street corners and risky motoring. Even boredom looked better in the city. It, at least, had street corners to lean on and drifting crowds to scrutinize.

And there was Harry, a figure blocking light in the doorway. Round head, square-shouldered. Moving from the light to the table, slight smile; a good-looking man, even a beautiful man if you studied him for long enough, in the right way, let yourself play with the possibility of his features shifting a fraction this way or that. The arbitrary gene had tilted him just off full-blown handsomeness. Nothing that character couldn't rectify.

Impeccably polite, he asked if he could sit down. Placing his jacket carefully over the chair back, the menu picked up in powerfully tender hands, nails carefully squared off, egg-white thick and clean. His presence was restful to her; no need to talk, she finished her cigarette while he studied the menu.

'Lemon tea and cheesecake, please.' What he always had.

He placed his cigarettes on the table; a solid gold lighter. In a moment, his full attention would be on her and never waver.

He liked all the periphery. The first time, asking her to describe the rooms; closing his eyes to see better, his hand laid lightly across the high glass of tea. She found the pure physical description hard to do. The place is clean and tidy, she told him, nothing special, a few nice pictures.

'They've got a cleaner, of course?' Harry cut into his cheesecake with the side of his fork.

'No. No. I don't think so. Me, I'm the cleaner now.'

'And the pictures? What are they like?'

'Like what?'

'The pictures,' he repeated patiently. 'I'm asking you what kind of art they like.'

She told him about *Guernica* and the lonely blonde usherette, standing by a red velvet curtain staring at the floor.

'And where is that?'

'In the front room, over the mantelpiece.'

'Are you sure? A cinema usherette over their *mantelpiece*?' He looked puzzled.

'Of course I'm sure.' Karen looked equally puzzled. What did he expect? One of those wild paintings that are all dots and squiggles?

He thought it clever of her to get so close to the girl. He

81

knew quite a lot about her already – birth date, history of the mother's career, some details of the divorce. 'What's she like?'

'She's a nice enough kid.'

'Talkative?'

Oh yes, Karen nodded. She had a page or two written out in her bag. In the beginning she wasn't sure when she should give it to him; he never asked. She liked doing it, working at her desk at night, describing the day's events, what she had seen, whom she had met. She even liked trying to describe people's appearance and character.

'Sarah.' He said the name slowly. 'There'll be things in there, too, believe me. Everything will be in there if you just listen properly.'

'She's quite an accomplished little eavesdropper, you know. There's a trick of the floorboards on the first floor, a way you can stand which means they don't squeak. Anyway, I'm working on the personal side.'

Harry's eyebrows were raised.

'No big dramas yet.' She was floundering a little. 'Not that, given the right circumstances, he, in particular, might not . . .'

'Might not what?'

'Well, you know . . .'

'Specifics, Karen. They're the most helpful.' The cheese-cake was finished, a few dusty crumbs left on the outer rim of the glass plate.

Karen smiled. 'Yes. I understand. Did I ever tell you I've a kid sister around the girl's age? Only I've never met her.'

'How come?' Harry was dredging the lemon slice from the bottom of his tea.

'My dad married again. I reckon she'll be twelve this year. That's what made me think about the birthday

82

thing.' She wanted to impress him with her professionalism. 'Actually, I read it somewhere, about a person who used to pretend to have the same birthday as someone he wanted to get to know. It makes people feel special, feel that *you're* special.'

Harry frowned. 'Your records are there for everybody to see at the university. Tom Martin could easily find them.'

'But he won't, will he?'

'Unlikely.' Harry inclined his head, implying: these people are so extraordinarily trusting, it goes with their innocence about human nature. Indicating too that she shouldn't worry, it would be taken care of. He would make a good shrink, Harry; discreet in all things.

She was never sure how useful she really was. His requirements seemed so basic. Names. Addresses. Who knows whom. Who phones. Who visits. Who sleeps with whom. ('Intimate liaisons', Harry called it, his eyes not meeting hers for a brief second.) He did not seem that interested in her painfully prepared notes on all the 'characters' of the house; Joe's secret wish for respectability, Lou's incomprehensible dislike of Rachel. He was much more interested in the mundane – the proofs of Tom Martin's next book, for instance. He had asked her to take a photocopy for him.

'Why? You could read it for yourself in six months' time.'

'This is much more interesting,' he said, smoking and scanning the pages. Later he would fold them between the pages of his diary, would joke about a 'little bedside reading'.

She knew little about Harry's other life. Two small children. He had shown her the expected picture, two nondescript little girls standing in front of a ghastly bronze fireplace. 'Charming,' she said, after the requisite three seconds. There must have been a wife, although he never mentioned her. He was clearly a man of rigid habits. He would never stay beyond five thirty, allowing ten minutes before he signalled to pay the bill, just in case there was a delay.

Once when he was paying at the till, she looked in a plastic bag he had brought with him. Ordinary textbooks: A. J. P. Taylor's *Origins of the Second World War*, a new biography of Stalin. More than once, he had said to her, 'I like my history straight. Ideology never helped anyone.'

He hated communism; formally, like an in-law. When he talked of it he placed it on the other edge of a moral see-saw, laid heavy already by pre-war Fascism. But even the little he said seemed to embarrass him. Harry was in some way inadequate to his cause, lacking not conviction but the means to express it. Except through this. What he does. What she does. What it means.

Given the right circumstances. She had said it to Harry chiefly in hope, in remembering the possibilities of the half-smile. Trying always to create them herself, the right circumstances; randomly, of course, without apparent will.

It was not easy. When she first went to the house, she and Tom were rarely alone. They met once or twice in the hallway, the voices of others echoing in the background or out in the street when she was arriving or he was leaving. He gave her no indication; she could see that rationally. Sometimes, she even suspected him of not remembering who she was, his nod was so circumspect, his smile so indiscriminately friendly. But in those early hopeful months, she took even these discouraging signs as a spur. Sure that there was some future moment of revelation hanging high in the universe, like Plato's ideal tables and chairs, waiting to materialize on earth. Her role was to bring the future moment into present action, not by endurance or patience but by an act of pure, subtle daring.

Given the right circumstances. She imagined them a dozen times a day, some small part of her acknowledging the clichéd quality of her ideal scenarios. Accidental stumbles on stone steps – the steps up to the house were in crumbling disrepair and the first day she had visited, she had nearly twisted her foot on the cracked slate. Or a body swaying the wrong way with minimum (maximum) force. He needed only to return her glance once, touch her hand once, in a certain way, to understand what was on offer.

Her hopes soared during the election campaign. Now they had a common purpose. They were with each other often in the slices of private territory that public life offers its participants: the back seats of cars, the damp, smoky rooms behind church halls, the peeling-walled hospitality rooms of local radio stations. These days he smiled at her often and with discrimination – at last he knew who she was. She could feel his need of her. Without others who believed in his campaign, he could not believe in it himself; in his eyes, it verged always on the ridiculous, the farcical. Once or twice he even took her hand, praising her work, her skill, her commitment. But in her heightened, almost invulnerable state she wanted to laugh out loud; while all the elements were in place – their flesh touching, his warmth genuine – the necessary motive for what she wanted was so completely absent as to render his hand as erotic as a dead fish on a marble slab.

The disillusion was good-tempered as long as the election was in full swing. The charge of the campaign was better than sex, she was fond of saying to Joe, who was fond of saying it back to her. The let-down came afterwards, when the post-mortems had been exhausted, the clearing up had been done, her own officious 'Campaign Manager' badge tucked away in her T-shirt and knicker drawer and she was expected back at the house, solely to fulfil her au pair function.

Then she could not bear it. Especially when Tom's blank looks began again, this time tinged with a gruffness and near-dislike. Almost as if he associated her with his own fatigue, his poor result. In turn, she almost despised his failure at electoral politics. *She* would have fought the campaign quite differently, with more attack. She would have given Old Dick a real run for his political money.

86

There was nothing for it but to go. To leave the house. To quit, as the Americans say with such successful finality. She would go to America for the summer.

Her decision was confirmed by an incident in the early summer. A warm day, she had come to pick up Sezz for swimming. Karen had to wait in the hall while the girl ran upstairs to get a swimming hat. There she was, staring at the dreary Picasso, now stripped of all its possibilities, when she heard voices on the first-floor landing. A man (Tom) and a woman (Rachel) – appealing, responding, affirming. In a tone of murmuring urgency.

'You do love me?'

'Of course.'

'You do?'

'Yes, *yes*.'

Both appeals were made by Tom, both affirmations sworn by Rachel. They sounded like two people who had not spoken to each other for a long time; she could not understand this element of their communication. At twenty-one, and a young twenty-one, she saw the exchange in terms of power, given or taken. That Tom would stoop in such a way to ask for love. It was demeaning. Equally, it shocked her that Rachel was not impatient with his questions but grateful for them. Grateful at being given the opportunity to concur privately in what was long accepted by the world. These two people, they loved each other.

Karen opened up the front door. The street was quiet, the faraway rumble of a train drawing into Euston. There she stood, waiting for Sezzie on the unmended steps, weeds growing up between the slates, arms folded in contempt. If she had come to this house in order not just to observe but to destroy some tiny element of their happiness, then she had miserably failed in her task.

The first person Karen saw when she returned from her hastily arranged summer trip to America in 1970 was Michael. Dressed in his old navy duffel coat, now fraying at the sleeves and the collar, he was sitting on an upturned cardboard box in the university courtyard, warming his face in the autumn sun. Since her defection to the Martins – his ironic words to Karen in the spring – their friendship had dimmed to the occasional drink or exchange of set texts. Even these rituals were performed with a reciprocal coldness of the eye, as if each understood that the most dangerous enemy is the old friend; worse, the old casual lover, to whom one gave oneself without commitment, if not hope; each now doubly spurning the uncertain memory of whatever tenderness they had once glimpsed.

Yet she smiled when she saw him on the cardboard box. Her American friends had lacked this sort of eccentricity: even their politics were wholesome, earnest; wholly meant and the less rich as a result. Returning now, she understood how much Michael was *particular*, and the more welcome for it.

'You're late,' he said, barely glancing at her when she stopped before him. 'Two *weeks* . . .'

'I was having a good time,' she said simply. 'And you, good holiday?'

He waved her away from her sun-blocking position directly in front of him. Only when she had obediently stood to one side did he open his eyes, a hint of mischief in them, and say, 'So you haven't heard?'

'Heard what?'

'That your protector is in big trouble.'

She thought he meant Harry, and her face must have shown the guilt, for Michael said, 'Don't worry. You're not the culprit this time.'

'What the fuck are you talking about?'

'Barbara. You remember Barbara?' Michael shifted the pile of books on his lap. Barbara of the half-smile, how could she forget? 'She has very unkindly told the authorities that Tom Martin took advantage of her ...' Michael spoke with a false delicacy. 'I am here paraphrasing the college authorities, for in these matters we lapse into such euphemisms ... and just before her summer exams, too. Which, incidentally, she then failed. Quite badly for someone quite bright.'

Karen's answering gesture of confusion jolted Michael into offering her his surprisingly solid box, putting his books carefully on the ground beside her. She took the seat in order to take the time; time to work out in what measure to hide and and in what measure to reveal her thoughts.

'But that is impossible,' were her final, chosen words.

'Why? Because it wasn't you?'

'Just impossible,' she repeated, ignoring him, 'because of so many things. Michael?' She looked up at him, searching for some echo of her belief in indisputable truths, but she could make out nothing on his shadow-dark face, for he was now blocking her light. 'Tell me from the beginning. What's the accusation?'

'Improper use of professional position. There's some obscure clause in the university code that covers it,' Michael said, as clearly and briskly as the putative lawyer his respectable father wanted him to be. 'She says he implied that the favour of sex would do her no harm in her year-end exams. He's her tutor, you see.'

'But that *is* absurd.'

'Yes. Everyone knows it doesn't feel right.' Michael was gently rubbing the thumb and second finger of his right hand together, as if testing and retesting the authenticity of others' speech. 'The problem is twofold. Why would she say it if it's not true? And why, more important yet, does he look so uncomfortable denying it?'

'Women are always throwing themselves at someone like that. Perhaps he feels guilty.'

'At an enjoyed flirtation, you mean?'

'Even that,' Karen said slowly, 'does not fit.' Martin was not a flirt. She had discovered that for herself.

'You know what I think? There *was* something going on between them – ' Michael held up his hand to stop her protests – 'which meant nothing, but she used it to explain her bad results. She's got a pig of a father, you know, who's always putting pressure on her.'

After a moment's silence. 'You know who put her up to it? That creep Harry Wells. Barbara told me herself last Friday, when she was completely pissed.'

Karen tried to speak. But there was nothing to say.

'More disillusion for you, I'm afraid,' Michael said kindly.

She looked away quickly, so that he would not see the processes of her mind at work: not disillusion, but quick realization, followed by shame, and then self-pity. At that moment, she felt she shared some kind of victim status with Tom Martin, tricked by motives previously taken at face value, hitherto unseen alliances. (Like a child not invited to a party, she wanted to cry out, 'But I didn't realize Harry knew Barbara *that* well.') She, too, had failed to see the obvious; human weakness and the true shape of forces far stronger than any one individual or group.

Quickly, she went over what she might have told Harry that could have fuelled his action, for she was certain he was behind it, the moment Michael mentioned his name. There was nothing, nothing. Choosing to forget at that moment her added jealous-dark comment about how 'given the right circumstances . . .'.

'You'll want to go round and see the Martins,' Michael said.

'Oh, no,' she said quickly. 'I mean, not yet . . .'

Some decisions are like that, made up in the head, inscribed in the heart before you know it. It was true, she could not go back. It seemed the most unlikely act in the world now, to walk up those few familiar steps to the yellow front door, ring the bell, step inside the long hall, which most often seemed full of a filigree, unearthly light best belonging in churches. And the faces? What would the faces look like? A few thousand miles, a few months had blurred each person to an outline most suggestive of a mood – Sezzie's ever awkward jumping; Kate's mistrustful stillness; Rachel's brisk, unmeant smile; and Tom himself . . . passing through and beyond them all, like a ghost. How could she answer questions from these wounded apparitions?

Still, some self-protective instinct told her she must put on a show. The next morning she went to his office on the third floor of the political science building. The pasteboard door was locked, Miss Churchill was 'taking messages'. Karen handed her a note, already written, in which the clumsiest sentiments of outrage and disapproval were conveyed, ending, as her mother had ended notes to neighbours who had lost their husbands or cats, 'Do let me know if there is anything I can do. Yours, Karen.' She had thought of adding a PS with some reference to Sezzie, but decided against it: too intimate. In such extreme circumstances, she remained what she had always been: the outsider, the stranger.

The case was heard and settled in under a fortnight, settled being the right term for the obscure wording of the adjudicating panel who found, in the case of Thomas Elgar Martin and Barbara Christine Ford, no technical breach of duties and responsibilities of a member of the university teaching staff by the former in respect of the latter. (Karen could see Michael's wry smile at the pomposity of the language.) The private, distorted word, scattered by Barbara herself and Harry Wells, who some now saw as her mentor, even lover, was that the director had called both parties into his office separately, telling the young woman that some of the panel felt more strongly about her case than they could publicly admit. Barbara Ford was permitted to retake her second-year exams, on a cold, late October morning, this time passing, but by only the narrowest of margins.

The same source gave an account of the director's meeting with Tom Martin in which strong words were exchanged, principally on the director's part: words about the moral responsibility of tutor to tutee, keeping inappropriate emotions out of the teaching situation and so on. An exchange which no one who knew the two men could believe for a moment. The director was generally considered the intellectual and moral inferior of many of his staff, possessing instead an administrative genius for time-tabling, the acquisition of second-hand office equipment by the vanload and playing politics with the great and the good who were supporting his pet project for the purchase and refurbishment of several Victorian terraced houses near the main university site. That he should, even within his own status-inflated terms, dare to lecture a colleague like Tom Martin on questions other than filing cabinets and induction courses seemed extraordinary to some listeners.

Karen never spoke to Tom Martin again, girding herself for the right words when they passed in the street one November night. But he did not recognize her, benignly passing an inch from her bulky red-wool shoulder. Inevitably, he was talked of as a broken man, but Karen saw this as the lazy shorthand of gossip. What had been stolen from him was the future – quite enough in itself: the glow of confidence he had thrown off in the lecture hall that first day, a confidence that came not just from what he had done but from what he still promised to do. They had all loved him because of where he would take them. Now they shunned him because he reminded them of human weakness, a weakness all the more recognizable for being shared by them, inscribed in their own possible future. His very stoicism, his determination to continue doing just what he had always done, academically at least, wounded them the more. Some drama, some flair for fighting on his own personal behalf as convincingly as he had fought for his ideas, would have embarrassed them less than his quiet acceptance of ambiguous chidings by lesser men.

Not a broken man, no. But changed, robbed; a stealing unseen even by himself. Karen was more affected by the gossips than she knew, for she, too, ringed the minor changes into major ones. That night when he did not recognize her, she saw him differently; saw his once imposing height not as an ever upward reaching towards greater things but as an unnecessary imposition, a dragging down to the ground. Karen could even see the promise of a stoop in later life. So, too, the grey hair was no longer dignity, premature wisdom; it was sadness and loss written into the body's very cells.

Karen North was not a poet. She read little that was not worldly or practical; the metaphysical, the expressive left her cold. But this did not mean there were not words for what she felt seeing Tom Martin walk down that dark London street, alone, neither rushing nor lingering, blind thoughts unknowingly fixed on what had been or could not be. If she had known the words, she would have said to herself at that first ever tentatively unselfish moment:

> *That is not what I meant at all.*
> *That is not it, at all.*

PART THREE

Summer 1984

And Sarah grew up – tall and clear-skinned – with the shadow of Tom's fate hanging over her, its consequences stalking her, marking the boundaries whichever way she turned. The 'crowds', as Rachel now sarcastically called them, had fallen away. They were left to get on with an ordinary life that had once promised to be extraordinary, if only in the worldly sense. For the adults it was bearable, maybe even pleasurable. They remembered what had gone before, could pick up the threads of a previous experience without too much disruption. For Kate and Jack, Tom's 'fame' quickly became just an episode in their childhood, an episode that passed away without their much noticing it. This was, perhaps, as much a matter of temperament as age. In particular, Kate never lost the child's arrogance that assumes itself the centre of the world. By young adulthood this had transmuted into an ordinary self-centredness; nothing very important would ever happen far from where she was. But for Sarah – this, too, a matter of temperament – the changes wounded and retarded her. Without knowing it consciously, she was, during adolescence, denied the experience of a world presumed stable, because she had, so early on, witnessed its instability, experienced untrustworthiness at its core. (Twice over, if you count the story of her mother.) By twelve, she had seen what power and the promise of power attract: the 'crowds', yes, and the special smiles for those associated with such luck and grace, and the odd, intense interest shown by strangers in nothing much at all. (Grown-up amusement at her spelling skills now fell into this category, and she dropped the practice abruptly in the year after Karen's departure.) By thirteen, she had seen what the desertion of the promise of power means: the gleam of shame in others' eyes, as if they – or she – had been caught stealing, or someone had died; as if the very sight of her, a minor figure in the drama, was a burden or a reminder of their own fickleness. And so she oscillated within herself between wanting to please them – by disappearing – and hatred of what they represented, what memories they brought forth.

One eye was always trained on Tom for signs of his suffering. These were oblique to any but the most sensitive eye or heart. Now, when he left the house to go to work, she did not feel the envy or the disappointment of the child left behind, but pure relief that he had a function in the outside world. If Miss Churchill, his secretary, rang – worried, irritated, fussy – Sarah felt profound gratitude at the idea of *place*. That somebody, somewhere wanted him, needed him. All through puberty, it was she who played the part of anxious watcher. Like the parent urging the child to complete their homework, she would often pop her head round Tom's study door late at night and see how he was doing, kiss his ever distracted left ear goodnight. A new book was in the making and each night she watched for a few minutes as he slowly traced out the argument in spongy black ink, the handwriting as beautiful as ever. Later, in bed, she worried about it. In a recurring nightmare, the manuscript, bound together with red ribbon, fell into a deep ravine and was never rescued; a party of travellers riding along the top of the ravine like old-fashioned cowboys – Karen North among them, in a stetson – did not bother to look down as the tight wad of papers spun into the green valley below. They kept on moving, eager to reach some new destination.

Tom's book was published in 1974, just after Sarah's sixteenth birthday. Her birthday night was spent stuffing press releases into snow-blind white envelopes. Again and again, Sarah read the catch lines, written by Rachel's sister, Penny, an astute public relations woman, that defined and distorted Tom's message: *Leading academic predicts that the tentative age of care and the collective is dying. In the next decade we will see the return of a more ruthless individualism that will threaten the very fabric of our society.* But a Labour government had just been elected and everyone was talking hopefully. The derision at 'Martin's backward-looking pessimism' came not from the expected establishment, who had always attacked him and whose sallies they had come, as a family, to enjoy, but from old political friends who now labelled him out of touch.

Tom smiled at the reviews. He treated every word written about his work as a contribution to a long, deep, many-skeined conversation. Rachel snorted at them and banged heavy objects – irons, jugs, ashtrays – from one side of the room to the other. The younger ones ignored them entirely or read half-sentences over someone's shoulder and then shrugged. Only Sarah sat on the big living-room couch, reading and rereading with an inch-long gash of anxiety between her eyebrows, knowing that the dream of the ravine and the travellers had come true; feeling, once again, in some way responsible for what had happened.

Yet the open secret of the house all those years was that it was she who had most changed; she who had turned from a lively, outgoing little girl into an inward-looking adolescent. Sarah knew that they put it down to Karen North, her abrupt abandonment of them all. Occasionally,

Rachel could be heard fulminating against people 'who pick up friendships and drop them, whimsically, with no thought for others'. Although no name was mentioned, it was understood that some portion of this remark was aimed at Karen's erratic behaviour. Sarah merely glared at the comment. Karen was *her* friend, *her* story; she resented it becoming part of what had happened to them all, one thread in the common tale.

This very pride prevented her from asking openly about what had happened to her friend, where she had gone, what she was doing. No one spoke easily of her. The odd item of hers that had been found in the hall or the living room – a hairbrush, a lip salve, an unopened packet of unfiltered cigarettes – had once, long ago, been bundled into a plastic bag, handed to a fellow student. Without words.

The facts were picked up slowly and painfully, piece by piece. Karen had completed her degree, gaining a respectable two-one, and had then left London: a second vanishing. A few years later, Sarah overheard Joe, who still faithfully visited, telling Tom that a mutual friend had met Karen North on a street in Bristol. According to this witness report, she was 'all involved in Third World stuff'. A bare six words used, nothing more. It satisfied Tom and Joe, who, nodding in oblique recognition, moved on to some new subject. If only, Sarah thought, sitting on the stairs, it had been one of Rachel's friends reporting back. Then, at least, there would have been details: not just of actions but of atmosphere; what Karen looked like, hair long or short; her prospects of happiness in love or friendship. They might even have asked the right questions: asked if she ever thought of her old life or wondered how her old friends were. None of them would have done what the men did: picked her up and dropped her, one-dimensional, into the street of a faraway city, there to walk away into 'Third World stuff'.

It always puzzled Sarah when she heard people talk about the metaphorical or literal dead, the assumption on behalf of the speaker and the spoken-to that figures in our past should be moved beyond, the surprise on someone's face when they hear themselves say, 'Do you know? I still think of her every day.' The answering look confirming that this is, indeed, strange. The assumption that those whose faces and voices are no longer before us on a daily basis fade, tail away. Stop existing for us, as so they should. The robustness of it! The sheer common sense! The pride on the faces of those who can put it – whatever 'it' might be – behind them!

At fifteen, seventeen, nineteen Sarah did not believe it. Everywhere she looked she saw traces of the unspoken; its manifestation most acute at the moment when a person thinks themselves unobserved. It was there, in a particularly forceful blankness of expression, one of a hundred old conversations starting up, speedy and relentless as emerging ticker tape. Internal combat. The worst sort. Over and over the old messages tapped on, circulating without point or resolution. A shake of the head, some muttering; these were the only clues.

Over the years, she lived out each expected portion of a young middle-class life; a turbulent adolescence, three lazy, intense college years at a northern red-brick university, the grey stretch of her early twenties. The gloom and extremes of the Thatcher years settled on her in equal measure. In 1983, aged twenty-four, she returned to London. Here, too, all the outward conformities were in place: a one-bedroom flat, a part-time job teaching English to political refugees, the nourishment of secret ambitions to write.

Yet for that first year back in her home city all she seemed to do was walk. A helicopter could have mapped her determined tiny traces through the capital, like a slug leaving its silver glutinous trail across a hall carpet. From Vauxhall Bridge up to Hyde Park Corner, through to Holborn. A bold straight stroke from Marble Arch to Bank; a curved bow from Finsbury Park to Aldwych.

It was not planned, her frequent arrival at Mornington Crescent. But if, accidentally finding herself there, she fully intended to walk up Camden High Street, buy herself a couple of records or a jar of face cream, she would find herself following her feet instead round the hairpin curve of the familiar road, until she could see Tom and Rachel's front door. A sign of their benign middle age, two terracotta window boxes sprouting purple and yellow pansies outside their bedroom window. Walking slowly along the pavement, hoping not to bump into one of the neighbours; standing in front of the house as coldly as a prospective buyer, eyes sweeping up and down, searching for cracks, damp, solidity – some sign of what the house knows.

Yes, the house knows more than she does. She is sure of it. Those small, high-ceilinged rooms on the top floor, that sunny, overstuffed living room, its shutters drawn today – yes, they know something of what happened. The clues are all there, if only she could read them properly. Watching her own face, taut and indefinite, in the dusty sheet glass of the downstairs window.

There were more ordinary reasons for returning: birth-days, Christmases, anniversaries of all kinds. So, Sarah made her way to the old house on a warm Sunday in July 1984 to celebrate Tom's fifty-sixth birthday. Bringing with her a pale Chinese vase that she had bought on one of her long London walks: an exquisite, rounded white bowl, daubed with the lightest touches of grey, blue and pink, wrapped up in tissue in a cardboard box that she lugged along the street with her, like a baby on the hip.

Walking fast up the left-hand side of the stone steps, now in a state of treacherous disrepair, she could hear Jack singing in the hallway. The sound grew louder, the monotony of it, as he approached the front door.

Neither of them spoke, but the greeting was friendly all the same. Sarah kissed him on the cheek. He didn't turn away. Rachel came down the stairs, carrying a pile of presents wrapped in electric-blue paper. She stopped still on the bottom step, poised on the balls of her feet like a graceful dancer. She looked at Sarah with open affection.

'You're much too thin, Sezz.' This comment, an attempt to suggest a parental anxiety she does not feel. And then, only then, 'It's lovely to see you.'

'Isn't Kate coming?'

'Nope.' Jack turned his back on them both. He still lived at home at weekends, treated the house and every-body in it with benign disdain.

'How come?'

'It's good, I think,' Rachel said, opening up the living-room door to unceremoniously dump her presents on the nearest piece of floor, shutting the door again. 'The mobile drone asked her away for the weekend and she went. I mean, *we* think he's a bore, but so what?'

The mobile drone was Kate's new boyfriend, Adam, a lawyer, with a fast car and a portable phone.

They moved through into the kitchen. Jack was cutting himself a slice of bread at the table. 'Hey, we're eating in an hour,' said Rachel, more irritably.

Jack buttered and bit into his bread in tolerant silence.

Rachel stood with her back to the sink, her arms crossed. 'What I can't stand about Adam is the leery approval he gives me. Like he's read a magazine article about how to treat the menopausal mother of his girlfriend or something. "*Lovely* hairdo, Mrs Martin." I mean, "hairdo". Come on, even my own mother would say "hair *cut*".'

I know, Sarah nodded, I know exactly. Adam had nothing to say to her, the serious half-sister with no discernible 'direction in life'.

'As for Tom, I don't think Adam even understands.'

'Understands what?' Jack's turn to be irritable.

'Anything about him, for God's sake. What Tom thinks, what's he's done. What he believes in. All that stuff.'

'He's all right, Adam,' Jack said in a final tone of voice, walking out the room. He hated them talking like this. Knowing they would talk about him and his life this way – the new girlfriend he had just met. Knowing he would not stand up to their compassionate, clever scrutiny.

'Here,' Sarah said to Rachel, when Jack had gone. 'Look what I got Tom for his birthday.' She put the cardboard box on the table, unwrapped the tissue and lifted out the Chinese vase.

'Lovely!'

'D'you think? I bought it at this wonderful, crowded place – one of those second-hand shops which look full of junk. Half-complete tea-sets and water closets and bad charcoal paintings and there at the back – this. Sitting on a wooden stand.'

'He'll love it.'

'It has only one flaw. See here.' She beckoned Rachel closer. 'There's a hair-line crack across the bottom.' They peered at it for a moment. 'I feel it fits, somehow. Because, look, if we both stand back' – they dutifully shuffled away – 'it seems to be part of the pattern. See?'

'Really, I'd hardly notice.' Rachel's first instinct was to dismiss problems, not try to make something good out of them.

Sarah put the vase back in the box and they sat down at the kitchen table. 'I bought it ages ago, in February. I've had it on my mantelpiece all this time. I think I got to like it too much. It weighed on me, almost. I'd look and look and look at it and each time I'd see new things. It began to worry me. What if it was destroyed? What would that mean?'

'Like babies,' Rachel said prosaically. 'You get to love them too much. They become a precious burden.' She rested her chin in her hands. 'The first night I brought Kate home from hospital I had her wrapped up in blankets in the top drawer in that old chest in the bedroom. She was so tiny, so fragile, I couldn't stop crying. The stupid say, "hormones", and think that explains it. Tom was mystified. He couldn't understand it all. But I did. It was as if, suddenly, life had held me to ransom.'

On the word 'ransom', Tom walked in and they both jumped, as if they were guilty of something. Sarah had an excuse for her awkwardness: the box containing the vase was still visible. She and Rachel shooed him upstairs again, while they got the presents ready in the living room, calling Jack and him back in when they were ready.

On this second entrance, Sarah allowed herself recognition of her first thought on seeing Tom in the kitchen. He looked older. He always did to her, these days. The hair was a fine silver; the beard, cropped close, almost snow white. He wore a perpetual small smile that was both defensive and distracted. It was as if the sadness he carried around in him, the sadness that any man of fifty-six must possess their portion of, was being sent out to them – for them to feel on his behalf. Yes, almost that. Sarah was having to suffer *for* him. She had understood it only because he had come into the kitchen unexpectedly. Usually, she had time to prepare herself.

Tom sat cross-legged on the floor like a yogi. He began opening his gifts slowly, methodically. A sober navy tie, tartan boxer shorts, black socks, a new coffee-cup and saucer from Rachel. A feminist book from Kate with a card scrawled, 'Forward into the Future, Thomas! Happy Birthday, Dad'. Three more pairs of black socks from Jack, wrapped in the same electric-blue paper as Rachel's presents. A book token from Penny, a paperknife from his own sister.

Rachel, who was directing the proceedings, kept Sarah's vase to the end.

Tom approached the cardboard box slowly, turning it around three different ways before finding the lip that would ease open the top. For a second, Sarah lost her confidence. She remembered what giving birthday presents had been like as a child; when, if her gift was a failure or ill-conceived, she would feel her apartness from the rest of them almost like a physical pain. As if it had finally been revealed – she was not a real member of the family.

Rachel noticed her nervousness. Squeezing her hand, too hard. The skin on her hands rough but friendly.

Even when the box was undone, the paper carefully set aside, the vase lifted out, her father said nothing. From where she was sitting she could see only the side of his face, the lips parting slightly as in a last breath. It was all right, she could feel it. He was trying to find the right words. In many ways, he had never found speech easy, not in private life. It came even less easily now.

The words finally chosen – 'How beautiful' – were spoken in a strangled tone. As if he was surprised at her kindness to him. As if it was the last thing he expected or felt he deserved.

Only then did she realize that he was crying. She had never seen him cry before, not even when he received the telegram telling him of his father's death. Not once during the 'troubles'. It was over in ten seconds, a quick wiping away with a middle finger.

'When's dinner ready, Mum? I'm fucking starving.' For once, Sarah was relieved at Jack's gracelessness.

If Kate had been there, they would have talked politics over dinner – a good old-fashioned slanging match about the miners or monetarism. Kate began a row these days as easily as she passed the salt or poured herself a cold beer. Words came too easily to her – imprecise, wild words. She was not afraid to speculate. If there was anything as grand as an ideology behind her attacks on Tom, it was what would later be called modernism; from this position, trying to push Tom into an equally crude traditionalism. What interested Kate – and she had picked up the phrase from some of her and Adam's friends – were 'new social forces'. She used the phrase quite unself-consciously.

Tom was certainly not a new social force; he belonged to the less auspicious parts of her new vocabulary: war-horse, Neanderthal, dinosaur. He believed in the 'old certainties', she would declare, as she cut into her tofu steak. It annoyed her that Tom did not rise to the bait. Political abuse had never wounded him. Much to her annoyance, he answered her on the substantial points of her criticism. And that wasn't what she was looking for. No, perhaps it was Kate who was the more wounded. For running behind these rows was her resentment at loving someone with whom she could no longer agree. Resent-ment at how publicly he had expressed this view – 'in your day' had become one of her favourite phrases. Or, 'I've declared UDI from all that ragbag of seventies causes' (this made Jack and Sarah giggle, a rare alliance). Her independence had taken on a new touch of hysteria – there was no other word for it – since she had met Adam. His materialism sat quite happily with his social con-science; why couldn't they adjust in the same way, her old parents? It made her only madder when, on the surface at least, Tom and Rachel welcomed Adam with generosity and kindness.

Kate *wanted* rancour. She wanted drama, some moment so terrible it would sever her link with the unresolved past. Diva-like, she courted it with increasing irritation. It had not come, nor would it in that way. There were other temperaments to consider.

Without her the table felt subdued, the family depleted and unbalanced in a way it would not have been if either Sarah or Jack had been absent. Tonight their conversation was cursory on public matters and almost entirely focused on the food. There was a shop-bought cake for Tom and no singing.

After supper, Sarah helped Rachel wash up and then paced around the house, walking up and down the three flights of stairs with the old restlessness. Eventually, she went into her old bedroom on the top floor. It had long ago been turned into a guest-room. *Guernica* now hung on the far wall, giving the clean, empty room a grim aspect. It was like a prison cell or a hospital room.

Sarah sat down on the bed and looked around her. Some boxes of her belongings were still stored in the bedroom cupboard. Rachel could not bear to throw anything away. For something to do, Sarah pulled out the box nearest to hand. It really was all junk – old school reports and a limp rag doll, poster paints and a chiffon scarf, pencils and a stretchy pink headband, some sheets of violin music, a lock of mousy hair – her own, aged five – in a crumpled brown envelope.

At the bottom of the box, among a mass of dusty rubbers and paperclips, the faint glow of purple glass on silver: the amethyst ring that Karen had given her that spring afternoon fourteen years ago. When she held it up to the window, it thinned out to the opacity of fresh ink; turning it away from the light, it closed in on itself, took on the density of blood.

Thinking of the colours of the vase now given to Tom, Sarah slipped the ring on to the fourth finger of her right hand, turning it this way and that, like a romantic young girl announcing her engagement to admiring contemporaries. She had never worn it as a teenager, keeping it in her bedside drawer as a token of her lost friend. Whenever she had felt sad or self-pitying, she had taken the ring out and looked at it. It had been thrown into the old box only when she went to college, determined to leave everything of the old life behind.

Without deciding at any moment that she would keep it on her finger, she was pushing the box back into the bottom of the cupboard without returning it.

She lay down on the bed and closed her eyes. She still remembered the favour she had done in return for the ring. Had that been wrong? It was one of the few memories of herself and Karen that she recalled with a reluctant shame. *I was only little*, said a high-pitched internal voice. *I didn't do anything, not really*. But it was Karen's motive that now interested her. Was it simply girlish curiosity and a touch of jealousy of Rachel? A student crush on Tom? Perfectly possible. That might explain the family's silence about Karen. It was odd that they had never discussed her or what happened so soon after she left: the dreaded 'troubles'. Such an open family, shouting and stamping about this or that. Arguments, even rages. Not this. Never this. Of all the years of their lives, that year was barred from discussion: 1970. They passed over it, like political dictators rewriting history through silence.

When she opened her eyes it was dark. She must have fallen asleep for a short while.

Downstairs she was struck once again by Tom and Rachel's eagerness to please. To please *her*. It was there in that first glance when she pushed through the kitchen door. They were sitting at opposite ends of the kitchen table, hands wrapped round large mugs of coffee, contemplating the vase, which was set in the middle of the table.

'I'm so glad you like it,' she said, drawing up a chair to join them.

'It's very restful,' Tom replied.

'Where will you put it?'

'In my study, I think. On the shelf directly in front of my desk. Where I can look at it.'

Sarah was pleased. She wanted to show it but she had lost her childish ability to cut across Tom's quietness, to chatter into his benign silence. These days his stillness had an impermeable quality. It weighed down on her, robbed her of confidence. She glanced nervously over at Rachel, who could always be relied upon to take the lead.

'So how's the new flat?'

'Fine, fine.' She racked her brain for some story she could tell them. She had noticed recently they liked stories about their children's lives. 'My upstairs neighbour is such an unbelievable pain.'

Rachel smiled encouragingly.

'Remember when I moved in, I thought he was a heavy biker? I could see him struggling with his leathers in the hallway, hear the noise of the bike at all hours? If only! He's just a tedious old gossip.'

Tom smiled, his head slightly to one side.

'He makes his own beer and he always wants me to go upstairs and taste it. Out of these big plastic caskets. I did once, it was horrible. And he's really into jigsaw puzzles . . .' Rachel whooped with delight. 'It gets better . . . He says things like, "Well, got to go, got to go ring my Mum!"' They all laughed. 'I mean, he's about thirty-eight or something.'

'Nice boy,' Rachel said.

Tom's concentration had gone. The women stopped talking, watching him without seeming to. His eyes had shifted back to the vase. He seemed transfixed by it.

'It's so rare,' he said, 'for me to see something that I really like.'

'Rubbish,' Rachel said quickly. 'What about that brief-case I got you before Christmas?' She was at ease with him as ever, as much herself.

'Yes, but *I* chose that.' He smiled.

'So you haven't noticed the crack?' Sarah said conversationally.

'No,' he said with interest. 'Where?'

'Just here.' Sarah pointed her finger towards the thin grey line at the base of the bowl, the purple of her amethyst stone gleaming in the evening light. Rachel noticed it, frowning.

'Ah!' Tom contemplated the thin grey line for a few moments and then said, 'Perfect.'

'Why?' the women asked in unison.

'Have you read *The Golden Bowl*?' he said to Sarah. Rachel got up from the table, a little impatiently, as if she did not want to hear what he was about to say. '*The Golden Bowl*. By Henry James.' Tom looked disappointed when Sarah shook her head and reverted to old 'lecture' mode. 'The central metaphor of the story is a golden bowl that signifies the rottenness, the fragility of a whole set of relationships. There's a point in the story where one of the characters smashes it – it's silly Fanny Assingham, I think. From then, the whole edifice can begin to unravel.'

'Edifices don't unravel, Tom. Wool unravels. Edifices crumble,' Rachel said with a mouthful of cake. Turning to Sarah, 'Dad's been rereading all Henry James for some reason.' She only ever used the word 'Dad' when she was trying to explain Tom away.

Tom's eyes were closed. 'I'm trying to remember the actual phrase that Maggie uses. About what smashing the bowl means. To her. It goes something like: "At last . . . my possession at last of real knowledge". I marked the page just the the other day.'

'Oh!' Sarah said brightly to hide her discomfort. This was surely Tom's convoluted, obscure way of saying, I, too, am weighed down by silences; his equivalent of Kate's bad temper, Rachel's irritation and her own covertness.

'Like the CIA,' Sarah added, for something to say.

'What about the CIA?' Jack had just come back into the room.

'"And the truth shall set you free." Isn't that the CIA motto?' Sarah's smile was now fixed, almost moronic.

'No idea,' said Rachel, turning her face against the conversation for some inner reason of her own. 'No idea,' said Tom, standing up in preparation to go upstairs to work. 'No idea,' said Jack, going to the breadbin for another slice of bread. 'Oh,' said Sarah, and changed the subject.

Karen North never thought about her past, and particularly not what she had done all those years ago. Occasionally, she woke at dawn with a fragment of an image in her mind, a snapshot of Tom Martin's face on that last November night in 1970 or her own handwriting on a square sheet of paper – on which was always written the phrase: *given the right circumstances* – but she had dismissed it by the time she struggled awake. Foolishness, the word floated across her brain, as she pulled back her covers to get out of bed, to fetch a glass of water, a cigarette. She liked it when she heard other people, in company or on some television programme, talking about their youth and exclaiming in pretend shame, 'How could I have done it! How could I have been so stupid!' It allowed her to think: yes, that is how we explain such matters, that is the box it belongs in.

After she had left the Martins her sole wish was to move on; to place new layers of experience over the old – a form of burial. There was a sober academic year spent studying for her degree, then a further ten months spent travelling. This was the period that came nearest to being her reaction, for she felt quite lost during it, without anchors in past or future. Drifting, inside and out.

And then a new life in a new city. The mutual acquaintance who had seen her in the Bristol street some time during the seventies, pinning her down in just six words, had caught the next phase of Karen's life more accurately than he knew. For in those next seven years, the substantial part of the decade, there was not much else in her life but the strange, functional mix of work and politics. She was working for a small research centre that took evidence of a variety of torture practices from around the world, then compared them with official government statements on their human rights record. The organization's annual report suggested labour of emotional intensity, an inevitable involvement in the worst of human nature that implied it was depressing work.

Not for Karen, who later remembered these years as the calmest and quietest of her life. There are no moral tangles involved in doing such obvious good – for who will quarrel with those who document naked evil, especially when it occurs somewhere so far away? Everywhere she went, first as a humble assistant, then as chief research officer, Karen found herself welcomed, admired, listened to as a representative of pure good acting against pure bad. This not only bolstered her moral self-confidence but acted as a form of unconscious reparation. (*There*, she could tell herself, as a mother leaning over a child's cut finger, *all better now!*)

She worked harder than anyone in the organization, a habit once acquired that was hard to break. Also hard to break, the habit of secrecy. Her attempts to make friends as opposed to alliances – or admirers, who gathered round her like a moth to the flame – were less successful. There were men; there was enough good sex. Casual connections that lasted for a month or two, maybe longer. There was even one man who lived with her for a year until he talked fatally, sentimentally, of marriage. But the very thing Karen North craved – ordinary, gossipy friendship; the elements found most truly in her relationship with the little girl Sezzie – now eluded her. She had loved Sezzie, she came to realize. She missed her terribly. At every opportunity, she watched young women of about her age, now; feeling ineffable sadness when she saw a group of teenage girls in the street, laughing, passing her, fading, gone. But unlike others who could draw on such feelings in order to make new relationships, Karen could not. It was as if that part of her had died. As if some ordinary element of the human machine had been taken from her — the simplest mechanism, impossible to create or re-create: the ability to make friends. Like an impotent man who can only watch in pity and frustration at what the flesh cannot be commanded to do, Karen watched a dozen bonds of trivial, fundamental importance being formed around her, helpless to do the same for herself.

It would be too easy to use that simple phrase, she put everything into her work. But in those quiet Bristol years Karen developed that special flair which often shows in those who do not have much of a private life, those with surplus time and energy. Her habit of dawn-waking brought her to the office at seven o'clock, an hour before the cleaners in their pink nylon coats. She was always the last to leave, checking and double-checking reports under the concentrated white light of an anglepoise while others double-locked the front door on their way out.

Her political flair was even greater, for Karen had some unconscious grasp of the changing times, what was needed to reach beyond the converted. Unlike most of her colleagues, she did not shy away from the popular. She did not spend her days talking only to those 'in the field'. Those years in Bristol were years spent practising, on junior news reporters, on freelances for the national magazines, on regional radio and television stations. This lust for performance irritated her Bristol colleagues, some of whom believed that the covertness of what they monitored, the quiet, intense suffering of it, should somehow be reflected in the style of the work itself.

It irked them to watch Karen become the sought-after, plausible public face of their small, modest centre. And then to see how good she was at it! Karen was always willing to let someone else have a go. It just happened that whenever it was Margo or Robin or Lesley or Tim, some funny reaction stole up on them when the camera light was turned on. Their swallowing became very loud, as if a cooking apple had lodged in their throat. Or, believing they had seriously reflected on the questions put to them on a radio news programme before replying, they would get home to find a message from their mum on the ansaphone: 'I was so nervous for you! When you stopped talking in the middle, I thought you'd fainted or something. I had to switch off!' For they didn't know what Karen had always known, as if by instinct: that a two-second hesitation in real life can be a fatal gap on air.

This painful sense of failure was further inflamed when they were approached at parties or conferences and asked, 'Oh, do you work with that wonderful what's-her-name, Karen North. Oh, I *like* her . . .' The listener's world was turned upside-down, if only temporarily, torn between simple jealousies and a resentful knowledge that Karen was, in a sense, beyond criticism. Doing them good, getting them known.

The relief was palpable when Karen landed her London job, in the late January of 1979. It was a coup, no one doubted that, for someone of only thirty to be appointed deputy director of a brand-new centre for human rights. The money had been raised by the great and the good, all those lawyers and businessmen and trades unionists who liked to operate in the wider sphere, get to know each other in the process. Cross-fertilization, as one superannuated old soft-drinks manufacturer described it to Karen, when congratulating her after the interview.

Nobody knew exactly what the centre was going to do. Karen laughed about the challenge of 'making it all up' when anyone at Bristol asked exact questions. The point was, they were rid of her like a shadow; a shadow of what they might, once, given the right circumstances, have been themselves.

The more perceptive of her colleagues – let's say Lesley, the youngest of them all, who had joined the Bristol centre last and was therefore the least resentful of Karen – might have noticed that she was not quite herself at the leaving party. It was a modest event. Crisps, peanuts and white-bread sandwiches scattered among the anglepoises and filing cabinets. Seven o'clock on a wet January evening with only a few outsiders invited. Karen made a brief speech with a distracted expression. Eyes and mouth, they didn't join up. She's lonely, Lesley thought, turning sideways to scoop up a handful of crisps. No one to talk to, poor lamb. There was scattered clapping at the speech's end. Someone came forward with the present, a two-drawer filing cabinet swathed in a magenta wool scarf. Thank you very much, Karen said in a dull voice. She had chosen the cabinet herself, weeks before.

There's something really wrong. Lesley knew it, with an instinctive shock of sympathy.

She was right. Karen barely saw their faces, heard their words on that night. She was thinking, as she had been for days and nights, obsessively, without respite, of her most recent train journey to London, undertaken in order to finalize plans for her new flat in Dollis Hill. It should have been a joyful occasion. Instead, that journey would haunt her for ever in nightmares. For years she would wake at dawn more frightened of what had not been said than what was actually spoken. In the thinning grey light, it seemed there was no reprieve if *this* could happen.

This: the man who appears out of nowhere on an ordinary cold spring day, the train weekday-morning quiet. For a few extra pounds, she had sneaked into first class, was settled with a cup of plastic tea, a chocolate bar. The muddy fields liquidized by speed and blurred panes. A man in a plain suit asking if he can sit with her, opposite her. Yes, if you must, the reluctance expressed in a smile. She notices his socks first, when he is pushing up his briefcase to the rack above, on the other side. Made of black, thin, shiny stuff. Marked by thicker black lines. A rapist's, a junior civil servant's, a salesman's socks. A benign smile, slightly laboured breathing when he sits down opposite her. She does not take the bait, picks up her book, a Maigret. To discourage him. A village speeds past.

Will you watch my seat?

Of course.

Why does she feel a peculiar form of attention being directed at her, a thirty-year-old researcher, from this older − forty, forty-five-year-old − man? Not quite a sexual attention but powerful, concentrated, specific all the same. It is familiar, this feeling.

The man comes back with a breakfast to match his socks: fried eggs the yellow of rape seed, bacon, sausage, fried bread. She holds her book a little higher, to avoid seeing the pink, brown, white elements, mixing in the yellow pool. When he has finished, he pushes the plate to one side, covers it considerately with a napkin. Begins on a plastic coffee. Could she just − half an inch, three-quarters maybe − move her notepad?

Yes, of course. Her mistake, to answer so quickly; recognition of a thread connecting them which he takes, now, as encouragement.

Is the book any good? I enjoyed the last one I read.

Well, I'm only thirty pages or so along.

Have you read any others?

A few — she stalls — And? — Very enjoyable, but very much the same — It is hard to hide behind a paperback.

I think — he says, quickly: the moment itself, a lunge, an attack that is palpably physical — I think I know you.

I don't think so —

But he rattles off dates and places, including her birthday, addresses then and now. A virtuoso show of the statistical.

No, I don't think so — she repeats doggedly. Sweat is beginning to prickle her flesh. A few seconds later there will be a cold trickle as corrosive as an electric shock, beginning from the pit of her arm.

Someone told me — the man is dogged, too — that you are working at the centre, here in Bristol.

But we are far from Bristol now, she wants to say, illogically. Nearer Swindon surely? An anxious glance out the train window.

Interesting work?

Look — a paperback cannot be slammed down on a train table to any effect — Do you want something?

No, no — he seems mildly panicked — pushing the breakfast plate a further inch or two away from her, towards the aisle: a gesture of conciliation, a brake on proceedings — It's just, I thought, you know someone I know — and she does know, before he has spoken it — Harry Wells.

Old Harry himself — she says with appallingly false joviality — How is he?

Very well —

No, really — Karen presses the point — It's so long. He was such a character. We were all curious about him, you know. Who he really was.

I'm sure —

His daughters must be what now? Early teens?

About that.

Well, say hello from me. And she picks up her book again.

He has expressed an interest in seeing you again.

It is planned, this. Of course. A deliberate attempt to draw her back. Somewhere. Get her to resume old insignificantly significant tasks. It must, she reasons, be something to do with her new responsibilities. She has made a modest name for herself in Bristol. Now there is the new job. She will be even more at the centre of things. For that is the point: access to the weakness of the powerful, the strengths of the powerless. It all amounts to the same thing. Information.

Oh, I've put all that kind of thing behind me − the tone of her own voice surprises her − Student life, its excesses. I'm sure you can understand. I believe in what I do now.

I was never that kind of student − he says bitterly.

Different generations, perhaps − she soothes − Now, really, if you'll excuse me − The book picked up as message for the fourth time. His faintly spoken − are you sure? − which she pretends not to hear, repeated in bolder form as they draw into London. The two longest hours of her life. She has thought of moving back to second class. But her pride will not let her. Sitting there waiting, waiting for his words of warning, threat. Thinking, it can't be this easy. To get away. Staring at the print before her, seeing mostly another kind of print. The small, tight, schoolgirl handwriting covering the sheets she gave to Harry. The loops of a ten-year-old squared off to shapes more knowing. Lines and lines of facts, assertion, specula-tion. The jokes, because he liked them. The attempt to be individual, to shine even in the most anonymous of tasks. Staring at one's own buried knowledge, proof buried in the vaults for ever. Proof she can never erase; the record of acts to which she will never have a moral, open answer.

What saved Karen was love, of a kind. For it was later that year that she met Paul Sandwell. June 1979; on the brow of a hill in her local park when she was out walking aimlessly. All pure, mown green, the hill was there to be climbed: a series of neat asphalt paths leading to its top, where some benches were scattered. The view was nothing extraordinary: concentric rings of terraced houses stretching out from the edges of the park to an indeterminate horizon. Streets and streets of corniced, pointy-roofed lives. She shuddered like an arrogant adolescent at other people's ordinariness; remembering her mother's fate, her own narrow escape.

Next to her, a young man and a child appeared. They may have been there all the time. A toddler, a little girl, with a round blonde head and pale blue eyes sitting quiet in a buggy. The man, brown-eyed, thirtyish, mimicking the child's reflection.

The simple fact of loneliness, disguised as sociability, drew them together. It was she who spoke the first words – 'Pretty, aren't they?' – about some flame-red flowers in an enclosure before the benches. He smiled, quite willing to play the game, muttered something about gardening, the outdoors, green fingers. She barely heard him; his unhappiness at that time made him mumble. It hardly mattered. Somewhere in that first conversation, a throwing of words between the separate benches, as casual and desperate as the throwing of salt over the shoulder after a breakage, they discovered the necessary. Enough to stand and start walking the asphalt paths, together.

There was no indulgence in her city loneliness, his marital unhappiness: the lines of the story were laid out and left like that, bare but unelaborated. Karen could see the man trying to find a tone to use with her, not to impress so much as to conceal. As she let him succeed, he began to relax, to shine. Her newness had warmed him.

He succeeded with her when she told him about her work. She expected the usual comments, usual at least among the liberal left, glum observations along the lines that we'll be needing human rights with this government. His questions were precise, tactical. Were they thinking, he said, pouncing enthusiastically on her jokey comment about 'uncertainty of purpose', of honing their work down to one, two, maybe three issues? That was the way he would do it – thinking aloud. 'Prisons, yes, definitely, rights at work and, let's say, women' – he was not so happy with the last one. Then, could they not bring out the wider drift of policy by pointing out what was going on, not going on, in these areas?

'Ah, but fund-raisers,' she answered, switching to a professional tone, 'and Boards of Governors and clauses in the constitution that bar explicit political work – that can make it pretty hopeless.' 'Yes,' he said thoughtfully, 'there are always these restrictions, aren't there?' But still possibilities – his look suggested – to make your point. Perhaps not so bad to have an apolitical image? 'It's part of the British character to listen more attentively to those who are not explicitly political.'

Suddenly, he let go of the buggy on a downward slope, dropping his hands almost immediately firmly back down on the bar.

Symmetry, she later thought. That was what brought them together. He had just transferred from a specialist journal to a national paper, a newcomer in the humming space of the newsroom. Like her, he had served his apprenticeship. Both were now poised, they hoped, for some break into success, both worthy and worldly, while modestly pretending it was not so. Symmetry of other more ordinary kinds: liking the same films, books, food. And politics: both of them practical, only loosely bound by the old heritage, wanting to start again if the old heritage was a failure. Neither was feverish or profoundly affected by the change in government, the ascendancy of a new radicalism, wishing instead to be cool, technical, imaginative about what was to come, their own part in it.

He was the first person she had met in a long time who could nod, vigorously, utterly without cynicism, when she told of watching the formidable Margaret stand on the steps of Downing Street – 'and forget all that rot about Francis of Assisi, but the *gutsiness* of her. Pink and white as a cake, but a voice like I don't know what. So sugary sure of herself . . .' 'Awful, but wondrous,' he added. Yes, she nodded, 'and it *is* impressive to be the first. Making history, however much people sneer.'

He was about to cut in but she cut in on herself. 'Most of all I like that moving-forward quality, the bulldozer, the bulldog. There's a lesson to be learned in there for women, the end of self-berating, whatever the word. Whatever the past, the failures, what matters is the present . . .'

Of the two of them, Paul had the more idealistic past. He talked fondly of it when they sat down on a bench. There were all the expected landmarks – anti-war stuff when he was a student, dalliances with fierce feminists in the early seventies. She wondered that she had not met him somewhere before. Walking among a bank of people through a London street. At a meeting. In the Martins' living room.

In a rare lapse – wishing to impress, to show him she was not a hick up from the West Country – she mentioned, casually, face turned away, that she had known Tom Martin, the family as well. When she said the words, 'We were close at one time', it was the vaguest of clues but he picked up on it like the good information-gathering journalist he was, quickly grasped the significance of her understatement. 'You're kidding? That man was my hero. I remember going to see him speak against the war – God, it must have been '68. In a church crypt in London. People were hanging over the rafters. My mate climbed right to the top. I thought he was going to get killed, had visions of myself having to break the news to his old mum. Of course, he had the best view.'

Like all memories of heroes, she thought wryly, his was as much about himself as the object of his admiration. He remembered those moments with the narrow, selfish intensity of a recalled love affair.

'You'll go back to see them, of course? Now you're here in London again?'

'I don't think so.'

He wanted to come with her, she felt it as hard certainty. That would be a story to tell in the newsroom: I met a woman in the park and she took me to old Tom Martin's . . .

'Really?' He sounded disappointed. 'True, the old fellow's not heard of much now. Wasn't there some sort of scandal?' he said after a minute.

'Really, I don't know. I don't know anything.'

'No, I'm sure I remember something. Whatever it was, it seemed to quieten him down. The last time I saw him speak, it was gone. The spark lost.'

Eager to please, he interpreted her silence as a lack of interest in the old heritage and now he, too, wanted to condemn Tom Martin to an irrelevant past. It was her first glimpse of a certain malleability that was not displeasing.

'Well,' she said slowly, 'I ought to be getting off.'

From the corner of her eye, she could see him puzzling it out: how and when would he see her again? How about a drink some time? 'What about tomorrow?' He pointed out a pub on the edge of the park – a friendly black and gold frontage on the corner of the road. She saw chairs and tables. Urns stuffed full of scarlet flowers.

'A Sunday lunchtime drink ... Come on!' he urged her, allowing himself a slight blush.

'OK.'

Until the moment she arrived, five minutes late, she half expected to see him with a wife, at the very least the child. But he was deliberately, flauntingly alone, sprawled across not two but three of the chairs, dressed in the battered outfit of leather jacket and jeans that signalled a serious sexual purpose. Pretending to read a densely printed paperback.

There was much less talking this time, all of it secondary. After an hour, she took him to her flat, where some of her Bristol boxes lay, still unpacked, around the bed.

Even now, as he took off his jacket, it was an abstract proposition. Even as they were kissing, sitting awkwardly on the bed like teenagers, she was busy with some other part of herself; getting up, walking away, thinking about practical things, regretful of his presence. Time stilled to a barely discernible beat only when they were lying together. (How easily the language is learned when the speakers are right for each other!) Realizing the passing of hours only when she looked up from her flat-out position on the bed at a changed sky; more than a passing of time

– a profound shift in mood and expectation; realizing it with all the bleary surprise of someone who has just woken up, has no memory of the dream.

How quickly the private – the first touch of breast against harder breastbone, the brush of lips, the clumsy turn of interlocked bodies that feels like a whirl through space and time itself – becomes the public: soft flesh to inviolable fact. Two lustful strangers in a London park become an admired couple; their vocations, aspirations capitalized. Karen North and Paul Sandwell. The Campaigner and the Journalist. If their picture is not immediately snapped on entering a conference hall or a party, then it should be. It will be. By the middle years of the eighties, he is talked of as an idiosyncratic but definite writing talent, a future columnist perhaps. And she, as part of a new generation of tough public women, occasionally quoted, occasionally pictured: bright-eyed, serious, mouth parted in mid-flow in the blurred columns of the newspaper.

And if some oversensitive strangers often feel uneasy in their joint presence, they can find no reason for it. Two such attractive characters with their interesting, separate lives, a spark of vitality between them that is lacking from the conventional many. Karen is never bored, blank-eyed at her partner's little ways. Paul talks too long, too much, especially when drunk. His sentences become convoluted, revealing an underlying pomposity that diffidence conceals when he is sober. She merely laughs it off, enjoying her own irritation.

For his part he admires her worldliness. Karen North understands power even better than he does. He describes, dissects it, while she wields it, bargains with it. Under her deputy-direction the centre is already gathering publicity and Karen becoming both more respected and better known than her garrulous, disorganized director. And if Paul sometimes seems just a little afraid of her, it is part of his persona, the man-child who seemingly defers to others while stubbornly laying out the parameters of his own territory. This, too, inviolable fact.

What the extraordinarily sensitive stranger divines perhaps is the silence behind the words, the words unspoken between the two of them. Words concerning Paul's ex-wife, Julia, for instance; a marriage already over when he met Karen on the hill but in some important way never left. There is still the adored baby daughter over whom arrangements must be made and kept; all the myriad outings, presents, trips away of absent parenthood. There is always a reason for a phone call. And if the phone call sometimes lasts half an hour and he emerges from the messy spare room of his flat where he makes and takes such calls, with a furrowed brow that suggests anxieties beyond the practical, Karen learns not to ask. She learns how to turn away, learns how to hide her irritation at his tangled private life. Thinking that if she had one real friend, not merely a hundred amiable 'contacts', then she could moan endlessly, joyously, about the 'Julia thing' and it would be done. Over with. Would not express itself as a quiet annoyance that drives him away.

She might even speculate with this (nonexistent) friend about other silences – two lost weekends in five years, a handful of nights when the phone is not answered at one in the morning. (This is their habit when they have not seen each other for a day or two. To ring at one in the morning and talk for anything from five minutes to an hour.) With a friend, she could laugh at the banal pain of hearing an endless ringing tone and getting no answer. Or his contorted explanations when they do meet: textbook answers about missed trains and sleeping on friends' couches.

She is not religious, has no spark of that kind of spirit in her. But at some level, in her dreams and depressions, she can connect his silences to her own, understand that they are part of the same fabric. There were times, especially in the beginning, when love made her reckless, dangerous even to herself. She wanted to tell him about the Martins, about Harry. Knowing Paul would understand that it meant nothing, that her main crime had been lack of clarity – direction – rather than pure malice.

The words were always about to be spoken, the appropriate moment arriving and then passed. The desire faded as love became a habit, too comfortable to be disrupted with shocking truths, and the familiar habit of self-protection returned. Paul could still comfort her when she woke over the years with the old, repeating nightmare. *She is walking along a train corridor. A tall, sad man approaches her. She thinks it is Tom Martin and reaches out to touch him on the shoulder. He puts out his hand to touch hers. As he does so, he turns into the man on the train that cold January day. He holds her hand tight as a vice.*

Karen wakes up just as she is about to throw herself from the moving carriage. Struggling. Screaming, no sound coming out.

She could not even tell Paul the bare facts of the dream, even though he pressed her with his habitual consideration. He has read a little Freud and Jung, is keen to find her absent father in there, her current boss, himself especially. She is touched when he says, could I be the man on the train? For he is often sent abroad by the paper and she has often spoken of her dislike of their early morning partings at Victoria – the breath of their kisses freezing the air between them. This late summer of 1984, he will be away for nearly three months, nothing linking them but scrawled postcards and a crackling phone connection.

'Won't you miss me, then?' he says, stroking her forehead at dawn, drawing her close with a strong arm, her favourite odour in the whole world, the sourness of stale sweat mixing with the sickly sweet smell of talcum powder.

'No,' she says, wrapping her arms tighter around his broad back. 'No. I mean, yes and no. Of course, I hate you going away. But it's not you. On the train, I mean. You are not the man on the train. That, I know.'

I t was bound to happen one day.

Sarah sees the man first, resting against a railing outside the tube station. He leans at an angle which protects him from the scorching heat of the midday sun, bathes him in a pool of grey shadow. When the light catches up with him, he shuffles a few inches along, moves his right forearm a fraction, to avoid the direct glare.

Shadow suits the straight-lined beauty of his face; each element – nose, mouth, jawline – caught perfectly in that first bold sketchline that defines him to the world, for all time. It is a Greek beauty grafted on to an English countenance. He wears it with neither insouciance nor an excessive knowingness. Rather, he has made it his own, by ruffling it, unsettling it – just as he now scratches the dark, tight curls on his head.

Sarah inches closer along the railing. She would like to hear his voice.

Within seconds, he begins to stir. The way he moves tells her: it is a lover who approaches, a known lover. There is none of that urgency of the new. Everything is expected; everything expected is pleasant. So concentrated is Sarah on her quarry, she does not take in his companion until she is already the sum of her ordinary, intimate gestures – a light touch on the shoulder, a quick white smile, a mouth parted for a welcome kiss.

That kiss. That damn kiss Sarah will wish many times later she had never witnessed.

Of course.

It's instinctive, to turn her face away from what is recognized but dangerous. To put a protective hand up to her right profile. To protect herself from the woman a mere three feet away from her.

Of course.

In the street. She had always known it would happen like this. A chance meeting in the street. Her right hand now protects her face as efficiently as a close-held fan.

Of course. She follows them as they walk along a stretch of pavement as open and sunny as the deck of an ocean liner, momentarily empty of other passers-by; they, oblivious even to this emptiness surrounding them. Nothing happens. No gesture, no obvious laughter. The woman does not lean down to fix her shoe or take the man's arm or suddenly gesture to a fixed point in the distance. Nothing happens. Two ordinary people walking along a London street in their lunch-hour.

Suddenly, they take a sharp left, walk up a bank of concrete steps, into a shopping precinct. The woman runs ahead of the man, turns to face him as he follows her up the steps; he, breathlessly complicit in the way of the acknowledged cigarette-smoker. Her smile is broad, delighted; a self-possessed, graceful woman in her mid-thirties. A woman in her prime.

Twenty seconds later, Sarah stands at the same place, at the bottom of the bank of steps. From this angle, the precinct up above, surrounded by high walls of housing, looks rather like a spaceship. Meanwhile, the couple have melted away in the dissolving heat. Sadness at losing them both so quickly. Then, glancing at her watch, Sarah turns and races back to the tube station, arriving there, puffing. Her friend Fran, standing by the same portion of railing where the good-looking man had been, her head turning like a clockwork doll's in dismay at Sarah's unexpected absence.

133

I t is reassuring, the shorthand of the blood relation. Her sister's first words on the telephone, 'Are you all right?' and her own immediate answer, 'Fine, fine', indicating all the richness of the unsaid. It is nearly midnight. Sarah lies flat across her bed, toothpaste still sweet and sharp in her mouth, the toothbrush flung by her side like a discarded knife, staring at the ceiling. Listening to a story about Kate's day, complaints about the mobile drone. Waiting until she can say, Guess who I saw last week?

Kate's voice fades away, stops.

'So guess who I saw the other week?' Failing to hit the light tone she had aimed for.

'God, you sound tired,' says her helpful sister. 'So, who?'

'Karen North. Kissing a man.'

'What, what, what? You're mumbling.'

'Karen North. Kissing a man.'

'Oh, *her*. Yes, of course . . . She must be ancient now,' says the twenty-three-year-old.

'Don't you remember, her being exactly ten years older than me, to the day?'

'Oh, yeah. Vaguely. So what's she got to say for herself?'

'We didn't speak. I couldn't. I mean, we couldn't. I was passing on a bus. Anyway, I'm not sure that I would have.'

'Why not?' Impatience again.

'Can't you see that it's difficult?'

'She was only a glorified au pair, for God's sake.' The ghost of an old class power asserts itself. 'But she's done well for herself, hasn't she? She's always in the paper. I even heard her on a late-night phone-in thingy.'

'You did? You never said.'

'Yes, I did. Well, I told Mum and Dad.'

'What was she like?'

'You know what these pressure-group people are like. Clear and to the point. Quite legal-sounding, even when they're not. I'm sure I rang you about it.' Not waiting for an answer, 'Anyway, she's just been appointed director of that centre for human rights. I might get some work with them, actually.'

Kate is every inch the efficient lawyer, although technically an apprentice while still doing articles with a liberal firm. Her professional route in life is clearly mapped out. Onwards and upwards, a phrase she and Adam love to repeat in mock irony; affirmation of the not-so-secret plot. In all things, she is enthusiastic, hardworking, affable. If she has any sense that she is not popular, an object of the unthinking love granted only to those who can extend themselves beyond their own interests, she does not show it. Maybe she thinks popularity is for the weak, the uncommitted. Like the ability to produce children, it is, after all, only the average miracle to which anyone has access.

Yet the adjective most used about her behind her back is 'smug'. This description is mainly used by her peers. Older people – the partners in her law firm, some of Tom's friends – tend to take her endless energy and volubility as a manifestation of high self-esteem. They interpret the permanent smile on her face as mischievousness not self-satisfaction, her impatience as good time-management, not mere insensitivity. The 'mischievous' label is enhanced by her dark, pixie good looks, inherited almost photographically from her mother.

The half-sisters in no way resemble each other, although many people lazily claim that they 'know' from first sighting that one is related to the other. This non-alike likeness is reflected in their life choices. For Kate is already hard-edged and worldly, verging on the insincere, while Sarah is proud of her awkwardness, her separation from the mainstream. To Kate, Sarah is a mystery – and mysteries make her impatient when she has no idea how to solve them.

Yet they talk well together, the sisters; love and understand each other with the inevitable fierceness and resentment of the family bond: loyal to the last even as they criticize or parody.

'Have you kept any cuttings?'

'Of what?'

'You mentioned seeing Karen in the paper, didn't you?'

'Oh, *her* . . . No, no. I never said I kept them, did I?'

'I thought you did.'

'I don't think so . . . Did I tell you my story about Joe?' They are back on familiar, safe territory. Joe, the old street revolutionary, now a senior lecturer in philosophy, whom Kate six weeks previously met at a station tobacconist's, where he lectured her for half an hour on Habermas and 'ideal speech situations'. They giggle again at the tale. It always surprises them how people they once knew have changed, how a young firebrand could turn into a tedious philosopher or an industrious minute-taker metamorphose into a television personality.

For the hundredth time they speculate on the relative roles of agency and fate, taking their childhood-to-adult experience as a paradigm. Was there anything in Joe's erratic behaviour that intimated he would one day bore young women silly on questions of the speech and state? Was his youthful madness being atoned for in his respectability? Did that spotty youth in the corner of the living room ever display a desire for performance while he scribbled down the words of others?

In passing, Sarah wonders why it is so easy to talk of the men but not the women. Within the family, they never talk much about Rachel, as if she is too central to the scheme of things to be dissected as a character. It is the 'boys' they settle on. What about Jack's new girlfriend? Is that going anywhere? Nah, fly-by-night-stuff . . . Kate, who is much closer to Jack, is especially protective, especially dismissive. She has met the girlfriend at a recent party: 'Pretty enough, but she overdid the lipstick. Even for me. Anyway, he's not serious about her. He hardly *looked* at her the whole evening.' If that isn't a sign?

'He is beautiful, though,' Sarah offers. Six foot tall, brown skinned, with those soulful brown eyes. 'Yeah, and he doesn't even know what a soul is,' the other one says, wistfully. 'And aren't his photographs good? The colours and the confidence he brings to their composition? The steadiness of hand and eye?' 'My own little brother impresses me,' moans Kate. 'It's worrying.'

When it comes to Tom, they nearly quarrel, the old tired quarrel, about how changed he is. Broken. Tonight Sarah begins it, unwittingly, by reference to a 'retreating, shrinking inwards'.

'Speak English, why don't you?' Kate snaps. ' What do you *mean*?'

'Turning his back on the world, that's what.' This is not exactly what she means. 'It's just all a reaction.'

'To what?'

'You know . . . to what happened years back. It really

changed him.' Her own impatience breaks out, in the cry, 'Why do you find it so hard to accept?'

'First of all, I barely remember the period to which you are referring.' The lawyer's tone has returned. 'And secondly, he was cleared completely. Given these facts, it can hardly be relevant.'

'But the scars go so deep! I think some sorts of personality can never recover from having their honour impugned like that.'

'*Impugned?*' Kate's laugh is bitter. 'Tom's just like a hundred other middle-aged men. He's settled down. It comes with the grey hair, the creaking bones.'

'You see everything like a cartoon. Simple cause and effect.'

'No, hang on, *hang on*. Isn't it you who's talking cause and effect, *you* who's saying that some long-ago minor incident caused everything that he is today?' Kate's voice is thin and triumphant.

'Yes. I suppose I am.' Sarah speaks slowly, trying to recover her true meaning, fiddling with the toothbrush by her side, flicking its bristles with the soft flesh of her thumb. 'But in a deeper way than you. You put everything down to age as if it's a natural process, unvarying with character.'

'And anyway' – her sister remains on the attack – 'you can't say he's not involved in things. Look at that full-page advert he signed about the strike. The bloody miners.'

'Well, what's wrong with that?'

'It's backward-looking, that's what. Of course I have sympathy for them, but they're hardly the future, are they?'

'Oh, the *future*.'

'Yes, the future.'

'You talk about change as if it's always good.'

'I'm just sick of it. Thatcherism this. Thatcherism that. Gloom, gloom, gloom. Things fall apart, etc. Forgetting that for a lot of people things are getting a lot better.'

'And for a lot of people they're getting a lot worse.'

'The Luddites were right to smash the machines, Sarah. *But the machines had to come.*'

Sarah would laugh if she did not also want to cry. They are dug into their respective positions: cartoon characters themselves, waving banners with simple written messages, the more complex stories underwritten in invisible ink. It is now after midnight, their voices low with weariness and mutual irritation. Yet they cannot sign off, not yet. Not until they have said something anodyne, healing. Asked to borrow an item. Delivered a small compliment. In the end Sarah takes the lead and they reluctantly disentangle, laughing, scolding, mild with remorse.

Sarah recognized him the moment she walked into the room. He was standing by the window, turned away from the murmuring main body of the party, absorbed in the slow-moving sludge of cars down on the Strand. A schoolboy canvas bag was slung round his shoulder, as if he did not mean to stay.

'Sare, Sare . . .' A blurred voice is calling out to her from the left. It is Fran, radiantly out of place in a bright yellow sun-dress slashed to the base of her spine. Her long neck drawing elegance from the intended sex-message.

With the muted hysteria of all party organizers, she is swinging a dark-green bottle in the space between them.

'I never thought you'd come.'

'Well, here I am.'

Someone filled a white plastic cup with wine, handed it to Sarah. The room was low-ceilinged, airless, with shabby, peeling walls. It was a lawyer's office, sealed from the outside world by sooty double-glazing. Fran began gabbling, speaking as people speak of dreams. 'There was the most terrible disaster with the name tags. For some reason they came back from the printers at three this afternoon – no, I tell a lie, it was three thirty – printed *backwards*. I had to type them all out again myself, by hand. On one of those fucking huge manuals. Next door.' She pointed to a left-hand wall, blank but for a wall calendar, as if Sarah had demanded evidence of her claim.

'And then no one will wear one anyway. Like you,' she accused.

'I don't like people glaring at my bosom only to find out I'm a nobody. I can't stand their disappointment, I feel I have to do something about it.'

Fran looked defeated.

'Is Mr Ahmad here?' Sarah asked. Mr Ahmad was one of her pupils. He had been referred to her by the organization hosting tonight's party.

'Mr *Damha*, you mean ... Well, I typed out his name tag about half an hour ago so he's been invited.' Fran went off into her dream again. 'Those old manuals may be huge, but they are actually very fiddly. Have you used one recently?'

'Not recently.' Sarah could see that if she did not stop it, this conversation would never end: Fran had the air of an obsessive. 'Listen, I've got to see this person.' Sarah jerked her head in the direction of the window. 'I'll explain all later.'

'Oh, I see.' Fran nodded, not seeing at all. But she was not the kind of friend who would ever assert her claim against the mysterious other possibility. 'Good luck, then.' She bowed Sarah through the nonexistent crowd.

The man with the canvas bag was now occupied, talking to a loud man in a tight suit and stripy shirt, the only person in the room who seemed to be wearing a name tag – ALAN FORFALL. As she looked at it, Sarah saw Fran's long, loose-jointed fingers painfully hitting out each letter, but the name meant nothing to her. She smiled at both men and tried to squeeze a way in between them, but Alan Forfall stood like a sportsman permanently blocking her access to the ball. After a minute of listening on the edges, she said, 'Would you mind?' in her best public-transport voice, and was finally allowed to slip round, to stand full-face between them.

There was no doubt, the curly-haired man from the tube station was saying, that a ballot would have legitimized the action. (His voice was just as she hoped; confident, even mellifluous.) Why were the union so afraid of it? When there were a lot like himself, democrats – here, he looked self-deprecating – who would be more at ease with what was happening *generally* if they could just feel there was a popular mandate for action?

'But why?' protested Alan Forfall, throwing a fistful of peanuts into his mouth; pet and owner, commander and subordinate in one. The union knew that they had the men's support, on the whole – his turn to look self-deprecating; the call for a ballot was just pandering to the national press.

'But *why not* pander?' The curly-haired man came in quickly with good grace, pleased with the offered twist. 'Why *not* show a little bit of strategy? Why always pit yourself against the world?'

They both laughed at the unintended pun, a moment's pause, then the conversation was resumed in earnest. Back and forth, the same argument with only the smallest variation in syntax, elaboration, examples. Sarah liked the curly-haired man. Even as he argued, he included her in his glances.

'And you?' He turned to her without warning. 'What do you think, Miss?' The old-fashioned usage amused her.

'Sarah. Sarah Martin. Well, I think,' she said nervously, 'that the most difficult situations are when you see people do the wrong things for the right reasons.'

'And the violence?'

'Well . . .' she began.

'On both sides.' Alan Forfall picked up the comment here, without reference to Sarah. 'It will come out, you know, Paul, eventually – *agents provocateurs* at Orgreave.

142

The men we saw throwing the telegraph poles, setting fire to the huts. In fifty years' time, secret minutes of some cabinet committee or other will show just three or four of them – and that's all you need – to have been a plant. And people like you will be so knowing about it all then. When it's all over. When it doesn't matter.'

Paul smiled. 'Spies and conspiracies. How convenient they are for you, Alan. Because of course they explain everything . . .'

'Nonsense. It's a fair if small point. History will vindicate us in other ways. We'll respect Scargill yet for his judgements and his predictions.'

Sarah detected a slight edge of contempt in Alan Forfall's voice. She guessed that his fondness for her new friend was chiefly personal; that he, too, was prey to the seductive manner.

Just as she was about to add something to that last comment – the falsely strident words 'I think' barely out of her mouth – Alan Forfall had picked up his battered briefcase and was tightening his tie. 'Well, better be off. Commuter land, you know. Good to see you, Paul.'

Then he was gone.

'What a fucking rude bastard!' The words exploded out of her.

Her new friend was already, soothingly, pouring more wine into her cup, reaching for bowls of food and placing them within easy reach until she was surrounded by a golden web of crisps, peanuts and cheeseballs. He was trying to tell her that Alan Forfall was a good man, a tough man. A certain lack of common courtesy meant less than what was at the core. She could believe it, and in some part of her she respected the coolness of the assessment, but she would not yield up her anger, not quite yet, her fist curving round a knotty handful of peanuts that had to be jiggled, turned and picked out individually until she was soothed.

As the curly-haired man talked, she studied him. He was as handsome close up as he had been from the short distance at which she'd last observed him, each individual feature good and strong. Animated by a self-mocking light in the eyes and a practised uncertainty of manner. A face that promised character rather than confirmed it. In ten years' time the boyishness of it would be faintly irritating. Now it was still a marker of charm, possibility; a refusal to be what he was, a fully grown man. There was a little bit of sadness, too; as if life had pulled him down recently and he was still struggling to rise to an old uncalculated nonchalance.

'So, what's your connection?' she said abruptly, generally.

'To here, you mean? Journalist – for my sins.' He spoke with false modesty.

'Name?'

'Paul Sandwell,' he said. Now she was frowning, trying to remember where she'd read it. Hearing her pupil Mr Ahmad's deep, guttural voice spelling out the byline.

'Ah-hah!' she said teasingly.

'What?'

'I've had your articles read out loud to me. Over and over again.'

He groaned with enjoyment, covering his face with his hands, while she explained that she used his articles for English teaching.

He liked being teased. Yet when she asked him, do you like it – your job? in that way that people of twenty-six do to people ten years their senior, with a prove-it mix of genuine interest and real resentment, he at least attempted a serious answer. Yes, no, he loved it, felt *deeply* inadequate

144

. . . an answer that became longer and longer, ever more twisted with qualifications and asides until they both giggled at his failure to hammer a mass of raw material into shape.

'I don't see how you write all that clear prose,' she said cheekily.

'You and a thousand others.' He took the joke against himself in good part, then suddenly looked grave. 'And what about teaching? That's a very responsible job.'

'Oh, I don't know. It's OK.' Like him, she lacked the words to order her experience into reasonable shape before a stranger. Unlike him, she lacked even the confidence to try.

'Tell me how you do it.'

'*Do* it? God, that's a bit basic.' She hesitated for a moment, then plunged in. 'Well, think of all the words you need out in the world. That's what I think. And then I pass them on.'

'Like?'

'OK . . .' She closed her eyes for a second. 'Like . . . a ticket for the tube, bread, margarine, meat, shoes, a newspaper, a box of matches, a pen, some paper . . .'

'Half a pound of ham, a book, some film for my camera,' he said, joining in the spirit of the thing.

'A light bulb, a pot plant . . .'

'Cigarettes, whisky . . .' He smiled.

'Washing-up liquid!' A light touch on his shoulder, in gratitude for his kindness in playing along. 'And as for your articles –' his smile became even broader – 'Well, to be reading a British newspaper, whether it makes sense or not, it helps someone feel less of an outsider.'

'It's a certain kind of language, though, isn't it? Not quite cliché . . .' He gave his self-deprecating look once more.

'Duller, hammered-over,' she agreed robustly. '"Shelling broke out in the northern hills of so and so", "The blah-blah government yesterday announced a state of emergency", "Disorder today erupted in the capital." I've become an expert in it.'

'Wish *I* could,' he said, leaning back on the windowsill, serious-eyed. The moment of unconscious decision had already passed – it had come, she thought later, at about the time he said whisky, she said washing-up liquid – and it was clear to both of them that they would not drain their snap-frail cups and say nice, ironic things over a deliberate handshake. What was happening now would continue, in some crazy, tired, continuous way, until the next step was clear and the next after that and so on.

Three drinks in rapid succession: her thoughts were as unclouded as a winter-blue day.

When she looked at her new friend he nodded – a tiny, almost imperceptible nod – and she acceded with a smile.

That much was agreed before Fran came over, her voice and meaning perfectly comprehensible but hailing from a faraway place. She and the journalist were talking, shop talk, people talk, and while he was deliberately boyishly, officially charming to her, he was at the same time deliberately withholding from Fran whatever it was he had offered or revealed to Sarah. She could feel it, hear it, taste it; the missing element was so resoundingly present.

I shall get my coat, she said, in the pale voice of someone about to faint.

They walked round the graceful loop of the Aldwych, an island where the architecture is grand and the roads wide, as if built for the triumphal march or the military campaign, yet permanently interrupted by the exigencies of the everyday: traffic, human beings. As if the island itself manifests a continual historical battle between two kinds of essential, grand intention opposing day-to-day necessity.

A glowing summer evening had given way to a thin greyness. It was that part of the day when the sky is drained and blooded, as if the weather has given up. From across the road, Sarah thought she saw Mr Ahmàd hurrying fast to get to the party he had long missed.

Just shadows.

Paul Sandwell was talking in a more daily way now, about his next tour abroad, to a country bordering on Mr Ahmad's. He was expecting to go in the next few days. It was worse, the waiting to go, than being there. Then he was just absorbed, accepting.

'What about leaving your life here? All that?' she said, limping a little from hitting her foot on the pavement.

'Oh, I've nothing much to leave,' he said.

'I'd hate that,' she began, meaning coming and going from a home base. But he was answering before she'd finished. There were a lot more dangerous places he could be sent to. This country wasn't dangerous at all. Only if you were in contact with political people.

Was he, much?

Discreetly, discreetly. Yes, she could see he'd be good at that.

She got no more out of him about work. He was making a big song and dance about their trip to a restaurant, behaving as if they were in a war zone, not entering a network of narrow back streets in central London. 'This place,' he was saying, 'is brilliant. You eat at couches, not at tables. More like a club than a restaurant.' Dark was dropping rapidly and they were surrounded by tall Victorian buildings, black with the grime of ages. 'Here,' he said, pointing at another low, dark entrance, but this one glowing with some mottled light beyond.

'You'd never find it, would you, ordinarily?'

'Come on,' he was saying impatiently, already over the other side of a small room, patting her a place next to him on a red velvet couch. Red velvet! She sat back, smoothed it with her hand. 'Is this a brothel or something?' The evening had long ago taken on the texture of a dream. When she went to the toilet, she looked too hard in the mirror and the girl looking back at her stepped into her own reality; became a second self, staring back, reproving, childishly scared, tentative. *Stop it, stop it*, said a voice from both of them. These are the games kids play. There's no room for such self-indulgence, small pretences of self-destruction in the world. Not in the world of Mr Ahmad, nor even in the world of Paul Sandwell or Karen North, those who supposedly report to us from the dark side.

Weren't they on the dark side too, in their own way? (She was beyond a little bit drunk.) It could never be proved. On the surface, they were all good if flawed, striving, doing the right things in a public sense. Why, then, didn't she trust people who did and said the right things when that was all that could reasonably be asked of a person? Why did she see as much truth in a facial expression, a minor deception or evasion, a missed opportunity, falseness of tone? Why and in what form did she look for some deeper proof?

Some part of the answer lay in suffering, she suddenly understood. This was what her father's life had taught her. And Mr Ahmad. Both had suffered, on a different scale. For that reason she trusted them; their knowledge of weakness unshakeable, unavoidable.

Back upstairs at the table, she was still drawn to the

journalist. His *seductiveness*. Yes, of course. Enjoying his sharpness perhaps more than his softness, a weakness written somewhere into the code of his face. And she could talk to him. He was so interesting! Had both an 'outside' and an 'inside', was prepared to speculate and reveal, and be silent when silence was called for, all with a complete stranger. Power and good, how little did the two go together. No, it was not that. It was power and good *and* worldliness. For there was power of a sort in Mr Ahmad – the power of refusal, resistance or subversion – and certainly good. How else do we describe a man who is tortured for the idea of freedom? Yet he and others like him were consigned to the margins, called to step forward only when the world deemed their gestures in tune with the larger mood.

So Tom had once done, his power and good coinciding with a need of the world. When the world turned on him, he had simply stayed still, while the rest retreated. (That phrase she had used to Kate the other night, a 'shrinking inwards', she was sure of its accuracy.) While handsome Paul Sandwell and his type stayed hovering in the middle of things, holding beliefs possibly but not losing jobs or hope over them. Never dying for them, certainly. A strong opinion expressed at a party perhaps, or in bed with a lover. An argument with a colleague or an editor, a certain way of writing a story so that it tipped, unseen, to the 'right' side, in terms of conscience. She was sure he paid a price – mostly frustration – for this empirical quietness, could take its exact measure, had no illusions about himself. But even so, it saved him.

And Karen? There were at least three moments at the table when she was about to mention Karen's name. It would have been easy enough. Each time she came near, she failed, understanding that whatever was between herself and Mr Sandwell relied on silence about everything else that nudged near to it.

Without doubt he had intentions towards her. Of that kind. He positively gleamed with purpose, his conversation becoming pressing, even coy. She must have friends of some sort? A gesture with his strong, good hands – wide palms, soft brown hair dusting the skin from wrist to knuckle. Oh, the flattery worked. She was still at the age where she wanted to know the answer to the slight question he worked upon them both. *Who or what is a girl like her? What could she do, in this situation?* In return, he offered scraps about himself: he had once been married, had a daughter of six, the great pleasure of his life. If there was anything that stopped him being a real war or foreign reporter, it was that. This. Her.

Bonny, her name was Bonny, a peculiar name for a little girl.

They left the restaurant; taxis were discussed. 'I'm going north,' she said. They agreed that they should share just up to Marble Arch. Not enough time to waste time. He assumed rights that came from the same place as the impatience of earlier. Pulling her by the gathered lapels of her jacket, like a gangster ready to administer a face-to-face warning; yet almost indiscernible, the how of the movement itself. As loud as a heartbeat to her.

It was done, then. She wouldn't have chosen to do it, this tiny act of betrayal. But she had and it gave her an enormous satisfaction she did not understand. To know that she, now, was the face tipped upwards to receive the lover's kiss. She, now, was the lover, waiting. Eyes closed.

A strange coming of age.

He was fumbling to think of something to say, some

nicety to tide them over. Or maybe a confession was beginning.

She stopped him with a gesture, placing her finger across his lips. Hush, not a word. No need.

'You really are quite extraordinary,' he said conversationally. And then, seeing Oxford Circus, a sudden avenue of unexpected space, rush past, added, 'I told you, I'm going away soon.'

'You said.'

'In four days. From 1 August until late October.'

'Details. Details.' She lay back, wantonly, on to the slippery ridged leather of the taxi seat.

'Well, Sarah Martin?' he said questioningly. For a second she thought he had rumbled her, had known all along. But the eyes were innocent.

'Write your number down – here.' She held out her arm, an old schoolgirl habit. Scraping the important things in ink. On her wrist, just above where the jacket would pull over. Make it disappear.

He was already busy, scribbling on the flesh and bone.

'Just here, all right?' The taxi driver had pulled back the glass. There was Tyburn Arch before them, the place where traitors were once hanged, drawn and quartered.

He slammed out of the cab, turned to speak a last word through the window. Her turn to pull him close, to practise that other old schoolgirl trick – the tongue deep in the mouth – an act of pure aggression that alarmed and delighted him. (Trying to hide the action of wiping his mouth dry as they pulled apart.)

Call me, he said, without a hint of pleading.

For sure, she said, without a hint of promise.

PART FOUR

Autumn 1984

On the night that Tom died, a cold winter wind whipped around the old house, unsettling dustbin lids and bending the tips of branches close up to the windows. A hundred times they brushed against the panes as tentatively as the finger-tapping of a nervous visitor, announcing a prepared entrance that never came, while those inside got tired of turning to see.

He had died of a massive heart attack, while Rachel lay curled up in her usual foetal position in the bed beside him. She had woken suddenly, aware of the new quality of silence surrounding her, the loneliness of it. Her immediate desire was to get away: jumping up and running downstairs, through the hall, out into the street in a floor-length pink flannelette nightie, banging frantically on a neighbour's door.

Sarah arrived the last of all the family, jumping from the purr of a taxi with the hard curl of coinage ready in her palm. Two o'clock. Looking up at the mannequin on the first floor. Looking up at the window behind which the doctor – the very same doctor who used to come to the wilder parties of the late sixties and early seventies, bringing his own spirits in a small, black hip-flask – was at that moment regretfully certifying death.

Downstairs, Jack sat alone in the dark living room, completely mute, as he was to be for weeks to come, while the women gathered round the kitchen table, drinking whisky and talking in overlapping torrents. Calming a little, they took it in turns to tell their story of discovery, enthralled by pointless detail. Kate kept unbuttoning her cardigan to show them a patch of sleep-stained old T-shirt as proof of her speed of arrival. And then, on the car journey here, she was stopped by not a single red light. *That's never happened to me before. Green lights all the way.* She repeated this sentence a dozen times. Rachel's sister, Penny, who had been called over as she had been called over for every family crisis since childbirth, told them she woke to hear the phone ringing and picked it up before turning round and discovering a strange man in her bed. 'I said, "Get up, get up. Get out whoever you are. Tom's dead. I don't want you here."'

Rachel laughed, her own story becoming a Byzantine joke, told against herself. 'I was like Jackie Kennedy. Don't you remember, Pen, the way she climbed into the back of the car after Jack was shot? Half his brains already in her lap? That instinct to run away from bad luck.' She was laughing again as she unscrewed the top of the whisky bottle. 'Whoever it is. Dearly beloved. In sickness and in health. Just get me out of here.'

'At least you didn't try and pretend later that you were simply trying to reach a Secret Service man,' said Penny, offering her glass for a refill.

'I'm not sure that's right,' Kate intervened pedantically. 'About Jackie Kennedy. She crawled out the back of the car in order to rescue a piece of Jack's brain. Put it back in his head.'

'Whatever –' Rachel swept her out the way – 'I should be grateful that there wasn't some tourist with a brand-new cine camera lurking in the bedroom cupboard, eager to film Tom's last moments.'

'What *was* that man's name?' Penny asked, her voice thick with drink.

'Zapruder,' Kate said quickly. 'It was the Zapruder film.' Again, no one took any notice.

'Imagine him in your cupboard, Rache. Filming right up close . . .'

'Right up my nightie, you mean.'

Rachel and Penny were giggling uncontrollably by now.

'To be shown ever after, amen –' the last words Sarah heard as she left the kitchen, to go upstairs.

All night, she sat in vigil by the body, crouched against the front wall, stubbing cigarettes out on the mannequin's chalk-white feet. She wanted to touch the body, but she was afraid. Every hour through the night, Rachel came up to the bedroom and sat on the edge of the bed for a few minutes, running her finger along the line of Tom's profile from forehead to chin, murmuring endearments to him.

At four in the morning, Sarah heard her say, 'You poor fucking man. Only fifty-six, you poor lovely man.'

At about five, Rachel was drunk and a little drowsy. She had perhaps forgotten or no longer cared that Sarah was sitting behind her. And she began to talk, out loud, to no one in particular. To tell a story, about how, when she was twenty-two, she walked into a friend's party, terribly pleased with herself, all dressed up in a little black dress and a chic black pillbox.

And she saw Tom – standing across the room. And she *knew*. *She* knew. 'Desire makes you like that,' she said, still looking at the corpse, 'certain and fearful of the impossible. He, of course, was oblivious!' Sarah smiled in the dark. 'I had to make him realize what he wanted. I always did. He did say, "You look like Audrey Hepburn in that dress." A *tremendous* encouragement. But I had to keep talking for thirty-five minutes near enough. I was ex-hausted. My friend said afterwards, "What were you doing making a play for that man? He's married, just had a baby." She couldn't see what I could see! That amazed me. Because you think what's obvious to you is obvious to the world. After my thirty-five minutes, I was exhausted and I thought: what do I do now? What do girls of twenty-two do in this situation?' Well, you can't avoid cliché, so you can only confirm it, with your own signature of style. Write down your phone number, that's what you do. I knew straight away subtlety wasn't going to get me anywhere with Tom, so I said, "Well, I'm tired now. I'm going to dance, which requires a different sort of energy –" he understood exactly – "but I want to write this down for you." I had the cigarette packet. He had the pen. I wrote down my number, but I wrote it down wrong. Not just one digit but two. The whole number was a garbled mess. I wasn't even drunk. He told me later he'd been ringing for days and getting a little old Middle European woman in a workshop in Finchley who sewed her own curtains and she thought he was harassing her, trying to drive her out of business. Thought he was some rival curtain-maker, only pretending to ask for this German-sounding Rachel woman. He was puzzled, Tom, but it never occurred to him that I was anything but straight. I always liked that about him. He never thought the darkest, the least good thing about someone, even in the worst times, those years –' she hesitated – 'when we were surrounded. That awful year, that girl in the hallway in her Little Red Ridinghood hat. Everything beginning with her. Everything . . . My own instinct, I had to trust it. About her and the other one . . . No one believed that I believed that "nothing happened". But I didn't even have to ask. I knew because of what happened to us. I was Tom's one great infidelity, I was his one break with the past. They say if someone does it once, they are more likely to do it again. I knew, no, not with him. He was too good a man in many ways.'

Sarah stirred in the dark. 'I didn't know what to do at first. When I didn't hear from Tom after the party. Breezed into his office a week later, thinking he'd forgotten all about me so what did I have to lose? And he took up our conversation as easily as if I'd just left him standing there, against the wall, awkward with a glass in his hand, while I went out to dance. He finds me amusing, that's all perhaps, I thought, watching his eyes closely for a tiny sign. Of urgency, desire, delight. Nothing that I could see. But then he told me that he'd been ringing and ringing the number on the packet. He wanted a serious conversation about my handwriting. Did I know my twos looked like sevens? Oh, I knew. From then on, I knew. Instinct again. Whatever the obstacles, I would get what I wanted.'

Rachel fell silent, a few long minutes after, saying slowly, 'But why did I give him the wrong phone number? Why give him the wrong information? That I never understood. It still worries me.'

Just after six, three undertakers arrived – tall men with dandruff on their broad shoulders and insubordinate expressions of habitual deference – to take the body away. Muttering instructions to each other and single incomprehensible words, approximating apology, as they placed the body on a fortified stretcher and began the task of manoeuvring the Professor – for this was how the chief undertaker referred to him – down the stairs, through the hall, out of the house.

Out the house. Past Rachel, Penny and Kate, who were now weeping in unison, a scruffy, defeated, red-lipsticked chorus, while Sarah waited upstairs, watching from the window, as they took her father away for the last time in a chilly, opaque dawn.

It was with the lightest, most innocent yet ruthless of intentions that Sarah telephoned Paul Sandwell a few days after her father's funeral and arranged to go and see him. (Each took the briskness of their brief conversation as an acceptance of the inevitable, not reluctance.) He lived on the south-west side of Hyde Park, on the sixth floor of a tall, white-fronted building that had, a century ago, been a grand bourgeois house with coaches and horses kept in the cobbled mews at the back. His attic flat had been the servants' quarters, three small, sloping-roofed rooms.

The living room was painted a functional white and furnished from good second-hand shops. It was messy, in the way that a home is messy when it is used more for passing through than for passing time: scattered with books, files, empty beer glasses, unironed shirts. Several thin patterned ties were dangling over a chair back. A large rubber plant was dying on the mantelpiece; when she touched one of its hard leaves, it came clean away, a glossy dark green, in her hand.

'I've only just got here myself,' he said, after welcoming her in. 'I've turned on the heating and I'm going to make some toast. Would you like some?'

'OK,' she said, walking round the main room, then peering out of the window. 'You're very high up here, aren't you?' The tightly packed cars down on the street looked like children's toys. 'Have you lived here long?' She had to speak louder. He was in the kitchen now.

'Years and years, it seems.' His head popped round the side of the door. 'There's no margarine or butter, I'm afraid. Peanut butter OK?' His voice tailed away in genuine embarrassment.

'Fine,' she said, then moved closer to the kitchen. 'I don't believe you live here at all. You've hired this place especially . . . and forgotten to stock it properly.'

Standing by the grill, he smiled defensively.

'Whisky?' he asked.

'Why not? I've acquired a taste for it recently.'

They ate and drank at a small table drawn up by the window, companionable like a married couple at the tail end of a quiet Sunday. Then he seemed to remember that he hardly knew her and the conversation became strained and formal. He told her a long anecdote about his recent trip abroad; involved details of a journey across a mountain, a criss-cross drive through a dusty war-torn city. She noticed he used the same phrases she had read in his colour feature reports published in the newspaper while he was still away; as if the experience was set on a template somewhere, could not be altered or refocused in any way.

After a while he stopped and turned to her.

'And you. What about you?'

'What about me?'

'What have you been doing since I last saw you?'

'Nothing, really.'

She could see from his face he was searching his memory for some fact about her. 'Still teaching?'

'Still teaching.'

'You look tired.'

'I am,' she said, and gave a brief smile. And then, 'I didn't come here for anything, you know. Just to talk.'

He nodded, with a look of relief.

'So tell me about yourself. Your real life.' She rested her chin in her hand and looked at him, thinking again how handsome he was and how, if it was true that the soul showed in the face, then his soul must, surely, have a lot of good in it.

'My real life?' he asked, in an alarmed tone. 'What on earth is that?'

The fear in his voice made her giggle. He liked that. All the muscles on his face relaxed.

'Well, you told me about a daughter. But there's a girlfriend or wife somewhere too, isn't there?'

He nodded, but said nothing more for the moment.

'A tallish woman, good-looking, grey eyes.' Sarah shut her eyes, testing herself to see how exactly she could remember Karen as she had seen her those few months ago. 'Slim, browny blonde hair.'

'How on earth do you know all that?'

'I saw you somewhere together. At a tube station, as it happens.' She put her hand over his, a small act of reassurance.

He let it stay there for a moment before getting up to clear away plates, fervently wishing, she could see, that there were more things for him to do. Wishing to regain some control of the evening. Coming back from the kitchen, he stood next to her and said, 'Actually, your ringing put me in a dilemma. You see, I should really be with this . . . other person . . . this evening.'

Sarah smiled encouragingly.

'She's working right now.' He glanced at his watch. 'But afterwards, I mean. I was going to meet her then. It's her birthday today. I was going to do the whole caboodle, meet her with flowers, take her to a restaurant. But after you rang and said it was tonight or not at all, I made up a whole set of excuses and promised her I'd take her out

162

tomorrow. You think that's terrible of me, don't you? You're shocked.' He gave a short, nervous laugh.

Sarah could not immediately absorb everything he was telling her, heard herself flatly repeating the words, 'Shocked, yes.'

The only things left on the table in front of her were two empty glasses, a trace of tea-coloured liquid in their bottom.

'Yes,' he was saying, with a puzzled frown, 'she's thirty-five today, or is it thirty-six?'

'Are you sure?' Sarah asked, because she, too, had to be sure. For fourteen years she had believed one fact without question: that her childhood friend was ten years older than her, to the day. She had to know.

'What can you be implying?' He pretended to be affronted, as if they were now playing a complicated but delightful game. 'I've been seeing her for five years. If anyone should know, it's me . . . Birth date, 22 November 1948. Yeah, thirty-six.'

'Yes, of course,' Sarah said, and then walked once around the room. It was the *strangeness* of it that bothered her: why had Karen told her such a lie? Had Rachel been right the other night in implying that Karen was something to do with what had happened to Tom? Is that why none of them had ever spoken of her all these years, because deep down they knew something was very wrong? *Yes.* Suddenly, she knew that was true. Knew that their instincts had guided them before fact. As a family, they had known they were being presented with only a partial truth. Unable to speak the whole truth, they had said nothing at all.

It didn't really matter what the facts were, after all these years. Tom's life was over, the complicated harm done long ago.

Over in the far corner, Sarah spied a pile of old seventy-eights. Big as dinner plates with burgundy and navy middles, etched with gold writing. 'Are they yours?'

'Yes,' Paul said. 'They belonged to my father.'

'Do you ever play them?'

'Not for years. I've a record-player somewhere.' He laughed out loud at his own disorganization. 'Do you want to hear them?'

'Just one or two, maybe,' she said, still preoccupied with her thoughts.

He disappeared into another room and she heard some shuffling and scraping, like someone moving furniture. Then he called out, 'In here!'

She walked through into a dark, cold room. The walls were an unfashionable womb-red, the sheets on the unmade bed a dark blue. An overflowing ashtray sat disconsolate in the middle of the floor, surrounded by more crumpled shirts and a pile of underpants that he swiftly picked up and stuffed in a drawer.

'I've found it,' he said. 'Shall we plug it in?'

'Yes,' she said, drawn to two framed photographs that had been placed face-down on a bedside table, as if someone was angry with the subjects or had planned to pack them away. The drawer beneath was slightly open and Sarah could see some objects that clearly belonged to a woman: a lipstick, a scattering of earrings, loose Tampax.

Paul was busy hauling out the old record-player so she picked one of the photographs up. A little blonde girl, her hair cut in a Cleopatra style, set against a bland grey portrait background.

'My daughter,' he murmured, then, just as she was turning the other photograph over, 'and Karen.'

At last, someone had spoken her name. That was a

164

relief. How strange to look at that face again! In the photograph, Karen was sitting on a deck chair, holding a white plastic cup, wearing a grey raincoat. She was looking up at the camera, smiling a lovely unaffected smile. The kind that cannot be imitated; it comes on the face rarely and it is pure luck for the camera to catch it, unguarded. The dark blonde hair was shorter than it was in the summer, cropped close to the face. It suited her.

'That was taken just after I met her,' Paul said, fiddling with the plug of his record-player. 'She's not usually that photogenic.' His tone was detached.

'She looks nice,' Sarah said, thinking that her original instinct about Karen had been right; that this was a woman who could be loved and trusted, whom she could easily love and trust still. Realizing, too, that it was possible to hold fast to a contrary recognition – one of trust and mistrust – without burdening yourself with too much contradiction or risking bad faith; that purity, the single story, is just too simple. So it was with most people: herself, the man leaning low down next to her, fiddling with the wire of a dusty plug, her sister, her stepmother, her father. The same story with them all: a catalogue of good and bad actions, petty and large, but no story without its share of shame or wrongdoing. Even Mr Ahmad, to whom she accorded icon status because of his suffering, probably had his share of malice and deception in private and public life. Like Tom, his suffering had only brought that knowledge to the surface, where it could be publicly viewed, commonly shared and repudiated.

Sarah put the photograph of Karen face-down with a tremendous sense of relief.

'Come on,' Paul was saying, with a suppressed excitement. 'I think I've got it to work. Let's try it next door.'

There remained one act for her to perform. When Paul's back was turned, she slipped the amethyst ring from her finger and dropped it into the bedside drawer among the mess of earrings, make-up, Tampax. *It was given to me by someone I did not know. I will return it to her in the same cold spirit.*

They went back into the other room and Paul picked out a record from the black pile, placed it on the turntable. The needle dropped into an immediate nostalgic crackling, and then a thin, high, wistful voice, singing of love and nightingales in a long-ago dark London square.

'Come on,' he gestured to her. 'Come over here and dance with me.'

Slowly at first, reluctantly, she let him take her in his arms, rested her head against his shoulder. The room was dark and shadowed except for a small side-lamp throwing out a ring of concentrated milky light on to the burnished corner of the table. 'There,' he said, putting his hand on her head as a father would to a small child, moving slowly against her, reassuring yet pressing at the same time. In a quiet voice, he said, 'I liked you from the start, you know.'

The way he said 'like' gave the word its perfect weight.

'Yes,' she said, moving closer, knowing that she deserved to be forgiven. For what she was about to do.

For Karen, that same Thursday evening is a cause for minor celebration, representing, as it does, an important step in the long haul to make something of her public life. An ordinary enough evening in many ways. She does these kinds of event all the time, thirty people in a church hall listening to her talk for forty minutes on 'Social Justice' or 'Human Rights: what Hope for the Next Ten Years?'. Tonight's meeting is slightly different, a political education meeting of a local party, known to be searching for a new candidate in the near future. For it is a public secret that the existing MP is dying rapidly of lung cancer and will be standing down in the next few months.

One of Karen's many political acquaintances has told her, 'This lot are keen not to appoint the same old type, white man over forty, two kids, etc., etc.,' adding with all the bounce of true conspirators, 'These are just the right circumstances for someone like you. Put yourself about a bit in the constituency before the selection takes place. They'll remember you.'

Given the right circumstances. She smiles at herself in the cracked mirror of the back toilet, combing her hair in its age-spotted glass.

The meeting will begin at eight o'clock. A well-heated church hall with hot tea and biscuits on school-issue dinner plates spread out on a table at the back, a dais for the speaker, a jug of water, three glasses. There are already twenty people sitting on hard-backed chairs and more trickling in as she bites at a biscuit, stirs two sugars in her tea, talks to the chairman. She is used to the kind of looks that audiences give a prospective speaker: wistful, hostile and expectant.

In these few minutes before 'going on', she experiences afresh the risk associated in standing alone, speaking alone. Those who dampen the risk through tedium lose the love, if not the respect, of an audience which understands that time has been robbed of its fundamental ability to transform, take us through from past to present. In the dull speaker's mouth, words become simply a means through which endlessly to repeat the same moment, whereas the fluent, daring speaker can rise above the cold night, the grey decade, bestow on the audience the rare, magical gift of self-forgetting.

Karen knows she will never be a great speaker in the old political tradition. She prefers the small scale, the intimacy of television and radio. Yet she has developed her own gifts in performance: lucidity, humour, self-deprecation, an ability to suggest she conveys a unique common sense. Tonight, she sparkles. It is one of those fortunate times when content perfectly matches form; her own ideas of where the old party, the old left, has gone wrong find eloquent expression in her, through her.

It is pedestrian stuff on paper: a litany of the 'issues' ignored by traditional section groups – women, race, the environment, even social justice itself if we are to include these groups – but the audience, many of them women of her age and older, love it. She can tell by the way they sit, palms pushed together, hands brushing against the tip of their nose, like proud, nervous parents at the school play.

Karen has moved beyond her usual remit, from the empirical to the abstract, from the exact science of her job to the inexact science of politics. As if she were a siren, latecomers are creeping in, immediately drawn to her argument, caught in the direct line of her stare. A young man already sneering – but ritually, ineffectually, in the circumstances – at her assumed liberalism. An old man in a fawn raincoat and a yellow wool scarf, unravelling it slowly as he listens sceptically to what she has to say.

Her speech over, he is one of the first questioners: she has talked a lot about justice and women and so on, but what about the struggle going on right now under their noses, the miners' strike? What's her position? Why has she said nothing on *that*?

'I support them,' she says simply. She cannot leave it at that, cannot resist adding her own rider: 'But they're not short of support, are they? Not really.' Some women in the middle rows mutter agreement when she makes a comparison with the nurses, or primary-school teachers. Don't they deserve our militant support just as much?

'I don't know,' the old man is saying. 'You and your type make me uneasy. There's a lot at stake with what's going on here, there.' He pointed upwards, as if they would all understand that he meant a northern part of their country. 'What these people need is our unequivocal backing. Now. While it's going on. Not a lot of relativist talk about women's jobs and men's jobs. If what you care about is social justice.'

There were some who would have argued with the old man. But not Karen, who is learning the emollient skills of the politician rather than honing the debating skills of the ideologue. When the old man is talking, she nods in great sympathy, scribbling a note to herself on a white pad as if he has given her food for thought. At the same time, she smiles at one of the women in the audience who clapped her earlier speech – a special smile of complicity.

Afterwards, she is approached by the same woman,

asked if she will come to another local meeting the following week; a request to which she readily assents. They make no secret of what they would like from her – that she should eventually put herself forward for the seat. Modest themselves, they assume a straightforward political ambition on her part. And Karen understands that she must now be as clear and purposeful herself.

The chairman has thanked her for the third time and she has gathered up her coat and bag, finally ready to go, wondering if Paul will be back from his meeting in time to speak to her before twelve o'clock, the last hour of her birthday. As she walks to the back of the hall, she passes the old man in the yellow scarf.

'You've got me wrong, you know,' she says. 'I agree with you more than you think.'

But his hearing is not good, his face sceptical as he leans towards her. 'Do you remember a man called Tom Martin?'

For a moment, she is completely taken aback.

'Of course. Of course, I do.'

'Died just a few days ago, poor sod. Didn't you see the papers?'

'Poor sod,' the old man repeats himself, shaking his head. Then he is chuckling. 'He fought an election campaign here, years ago. I helped him out a bit, you know, leafleting and canvassing. Foot-soldier stuff.' The old man beamed proudly. 'I was fed up with Labour back then. Still am. Hopeless politician, that Martin. A book man really. But a good man.'

Karen has blocked it out – her own knowledge that this was the constituency in which Tom Martin put up against the official Labour candidate all those years ago. All those campaign weeks of fluke hot June weather when she ran from here to there, handing out leaflets to the children at street ends. Whatever had allowed her to forget that? And how extraordinary that she should now be here, barely a week after Tom had died, looking to replace him.

'I helped him out, too, you know. Did a lot of work on that campaign when I was a student.' Karen is nearly shouting now. Trying to break through the sad, puzzled expression on the old man's face, as he twists the smooth yellow scarf in his hands. Listening but not hearing.

This will not be the last time Karen North invokes the name of Tom Martin in her long and successful political career. She chooses her moment carefully, uses it when she is among political scientists or sentimental old communists. Where the name is known, she is, each time, intrigued and dismayed by the reaction. There is affection, you could call it love. And irritation, a willingness to dive straight away into argument, a vivid shadow-boxing with 'his' ideas. A trace of sadness, too, among those who felt him lost to the world if not himself. But never cynicism. Never the tired knowing look that attaches to so many other public figures, herself included. No, Tom Martin is granted the freshness and innocence of Stendhal's happy few, an attitude she finds ever more enviable — even moving — as her own life passes; a life of far greater conformity if not ease than that of the man she once desired and betrayed.

EPILOGUE

1990

*S*he is famous now. Not as prime ministers or pop stars are famous, but good-works famous. Few stare at her in the street with the malicious delight that the truly well known evoke but some heads do quietly turn, words catching up slowly with the thought: that's Karen What's-her-name, isn't it? Who does that late-night programme?

I'll give you an example of her good works. The other day I opened up one of those endless mailshots that come to the house, complete with direct-debit form and gruesome photographs. In the centre spread of the main leaflet there was a picture: twelve of the great and good – MPs, writers, journalists – chained to a railing outside a foreign embassy in protest at its government's cruelty to dissidents. I am drawn to her unsmiling face; I could have told you she would be among the protesters. We have come to expect her there. Perhaps I follow her career more closely than others, have come to understand her own calculations, the rough balance she strikes between writing, speaking, practical action. For instance, in 1987 I watched with interest her campaign in a London seat, the same seat that Tom fought so fruitlessly in 1970. She lost by the narrowest margin to a young black accountant, a Tory man. But she is expected to get there next time. The gossip is only of 'setbacks'.

Her real forte, however, is television. There must be a shortage of intellectual culturally aware political women. Etc. She is some-times on two programmes a night. Especially the late-night discus-sion shows – I knit as I watch, so as not to feel I am wasting time – where they gather together four or five experts. Men, mostly. In their thirties and forties. Soft, round paunches. Little bald patches.

175

And Karen, ever slimmer, beautiful at the right angle. She has returned to the cropped look of the photo I glimpsed in Paul's bedroom. It suits her. Over the years she has learned not just how to style her hair and wear the most appropriate clothes — that is, clothes just like everyone else's — she has learned the other important skills, like how not to flutter her hands when she makes a gesture, how not to nod too emphatically. (What she does instead is wiggle her right foot, almost imperceptibly. I have become an expert in watching the fine trembling of that elegant, black, low-heeled boot.) There is a calculated stillness, to her body at least, which impresses.

A woman who knows her own mind. I noticed it most the other week, when the man sitting next to her, the foreign editor of a national newspaper, was gesticulating like a monkey at the zoo, his chair literally vibrating with the enthusiasm he brought to his argument, to combating the stupidity of his opponents. The more he moved around, the more ridiculous his words became, while Karen sat quietly, watching him with the faintest smile of amusement on her face. Totally in command.

She came to Tom's memorial service, slipped in at the back. Dressed in a sober business suit and tan tights like somebody's auntie. The service was held in a small church in the old Italian section of London. It was packed, mostly with people I did not recognize. I was reading, something I had written myself. I can't remember much about it; I was nervous. Afraid of making a fool of myself up at the grand eagle of a lectern. I had been allotted seven minutes and in the end I took eight. Afterwards the coordinator — for memorial services need coordinators, just like weddings do, apparently — said to me: oh, that was so marvellous, you could have gone on and on, no one would have minded. The very man who had rung me three times the week before to say, seven minutes maximum, or we won't get to the ex-minister of housing, who knew Tom at college and is going to read 'A Time to Love and a Time to Hate' from Ecclesiastes.

And there she was, watching me. I saw her from the start. I decided to pitch my voice at her, telling myself that this was purely a technical question; if I could reach her, standing right at the back, I could reach everybody.

It was not that simple.

When she looked at me, I saw that the ring had done its job. She knew something, about Paul, about me. And did she understand that the more distant past was no secret to me either? That I held fragments of knowledge, in my head, in my heart?

I said to myself: if she comes to speak to me, I will slap her or I will kiss her.

I will see when the moment comes.

The moment did not come.

Not then. The moment came later. We met in Oxford Street, a few months after the service. A complete coincidence. Funny, I always recall it as taking place beneath the clock at Selfridges. It was not there, not in so grand a location, but a couple of blocks up, nearer the Marble Arch end. Opposite a hamburger restaurant and a shop displaying pretty silk underwear and gaudy ties in its window. Karen was carrying a large bright-green plastic bag. I was not shopping at all, simply crossing the main road at that junction. A poetry magazine I had begun to write for had small offices on the Baker Street side. I doubt if either of us would have stopped if we had not literally bumped into each other.

She was walking backwards, perhaps trying to catch the time on the bronze clock. A man passing smiled at us, I remember that. And it was beginning to rain. I remember that, too, because when she turned her face was screwed up with light annoyance not just at the jolt but at the scattered drops falling on to her face.

At first, she simply stared. I saw a person who had long relied on some fraction of a moment to prepare the desired expression for the occasion at hand. To be deprived of that chance of preparation made her angry, I think.

My own expression was pure alarm. The slap-or-kiss option haunted me briefly, then faded away as the present moment took charge.

'Sezzie!' It burst out of her, the old nickname. No one had called me that for nearly twenty years. 'Can I . . .' she asked. Meaning, hug me, hold me.

I was a rag doll in her arms. A string of sentences spoken: how sorry she was about Tom, how important so much of what he had said and done was to her, how she had seen something I'd written, how good I promised to be, how Kate and she had met over a legal case — strange, I knew nothing of it — how good she promised to be, how tall I was. Did I remember all the things we had done together? All our talks?

She looked nice. Professional. Approachable. A woman in her element. Smelling of a sweet, musk perfume.

'You're trembling.'

'Just cold,' I replied, executing a dramatic shiver to prove the point.

'You know the most extraordinary thing,' she said, lightening her grip. 'Last night, I dreamed we were in a room together. You were at one end and I was at the other. It was a large, bare place, with hardly any furniture. I was walking towards you and we met in the middle of the room. And we embraced. I was so happy.'

She was excited, a faint pink flush beginning on her throat.

I nodded. I knew this was the plain truth. Already she was telling me the truth. That was the best and worst of it. The hum of connection beginning again between us. Love again, beginning between us.

'Have you any time?' she said. 'Just to sit and talk for a bit?'

She did not look at me as she spoke. She did not dare.

In that second, I thought about bravery. And foolishness. And this offer of hers: the most extraordinary compliment paid not just to the endurance of pure feeling but to ambivalence also; the everyday mix of love and hate, hope and disappointment in human relations that we are thankfully never taught to expect. And yet it comes so often, in so many of our dealings, large and small. Comes like this, catching us out on a drizzling day, round about noon, completely unprepared – asking for an immediate response that must be drawn from knowledge we do not as yet realize how to possess.

READ MORE IN PENGUIN

In every corner of the world, on every subject under the sun, Penguin represents quality and variety – the very best in publishing today.

For complete information about books available from Penguin – including Puffins, Penguin Classics and Arkana – and how to order them, write to us at the appropriate address below. Please note that for copyright reasons the selection of books varies from country to country.

In the United Kingdom: Please write to *Dept. EP, Penguin Books Ltd, Bath Road, Harmondsworth, West Drayton, Middlesex UB7 ODA*

In the United States: Please write to *Consumer Sales, Penguin USA, P.O. Box 999, Dept. 17109, Bergenfield, New Jersey 07621-0120.* VISA and MasterCard holders call 1-800-253-6476 to order Penguin titles

In Canada: Please write to *Penguin Books Canada Ltd, 10 Alcorn Avenue, Suite 300, Toronto, Ontario M4V 3B2*

In Australia: Please write to *Penguin Books Australia Ltd, P.O. Box 257, Ringwood, Victoria 3134*

In New Zealand: Please write to *Penguin Books (NZ) Ltd, Private Bag 102902, North Shore Mail Centre, Auckland 10*

In India: Please write to *Penguin Books India Pvt Ltd, 706 Eros Apartments, 56 Nehru Place, New Delhi 110 019*

In the Netherlands: Please write to *Penguin Books Netherlands bv, Postbus 3507, NL-1001 AH Amsterdam*

In Germany: Please write to *Penguin Books Deutschland GmbH, Metzlerstrasse 26, 60594 Frankfurt am Main*

In Spain: Please write to *Penguin Books S. A., Bravo Murillo 19, 1° B, 28015 Madrid*

In Italy: Please write to *Penguin Italia s.r.l., Via Felice Casati 20, I–20124 Milano*

In France: Please write to *Penguin France S. A., 17 rue Lejeune, F–31000 Toulouse*

In Japan: Please write to *Penguin Books Japan, Ishikiribashi Building, 2–5–4, Suido, Bunkyo-ku, Tokyo 112*

In Greece: Please write to *Penguin Hellas Ltd, Dimocritou 3, GR–106 71 Athens*

In South Africa: Please write to *Longman Penguin Southern Africa (Pty) Ltd, Private Bag X08, Bertsham 2013*

READ MORE IN PENGUIN

A CHOICE OF FICTION

Felicia's Journey William Trevor
Winner of the 1994 Whitbread Book of the Year Award

Vividly and with heart-aching insight William Trevor traces the desperate plight of a young Irish girl scouring the post-industrial Midlands for her lover. Unable to find Johnny, she is, instead, found by Mr Hilditch, pudgy canteen manager, collecter and befriender of homeless young girls.

The Eye in the Door Pat Barker

'Barker weaves fact and fiction to spellbinding effect, conjuring up the vastness of the First World War through its chilling impact on the minds of the men who endured it ... a startlingly original work of fiction ... it extends the boundaries not only of the anti-war novel, but of fiction generally' – *Sunday Telegraph*

The Heart of It Barry Hines

Cal Rickards, a successful scriptwriter, is forced to return to the Yorkshire mining town of his youth when his father, a leading voice in the 1980s miners' strike, suddenly becomes ill. Gradually, as Cal delves into his family's past and faces unsettling memories, he comes to reassess his own future.

Dr Haggard's Disease Patrick McGrath

'The reader is compellingly drawn into Dr Haggard's life as it begins to unfold through episodic flashbacks ... It is a beautiful story, impressively told, with a restraint and a grasp of technicality that command belief, and a lyricism that gives the description of the love affair the sort of epic quality rarely found these days' – *The Times*

A Place I've Never Been David Leavitt

'Wise, witty and cunningly fuelled by narrative ... another high calibre collection by an unnervingly mature young writer' – *Sunday Times*. 'Leavitt can make a world at a stroke and people it with convincing characters ... humane, touching and beautifully written' – *Observer*

READ MORE IN PENGUIN

A CHOICE OF FICTION

Simeon's Bride Alison G. Taylor

In the North Wales village of Salem, beauty and poverty, suspicion and superstition, walk hand in hand, and police and criminals know each other only too well. But nobody admits to knowing anything about the woman found hanged in the woods . . .

The Afterlife and Other Stories John Updike

'Here we have an Updike afterlife of revisitings, uneasy remarryings, leave-takings, and stocktakings . . . when he gets his hands on the short story the master can do no wrong' – *The New York Review of Books*

Signals of Distress Jim Crace

In the winter of 1836 the *Belle of Wilmington* is wrecked off Wherrytown. The Captain and his American sailors flirt, drink, brawl, repair the damage to their ship . . . and inflict fresh damage on the town. Another visitor marooned far from home is Aymer Smith, a man brimming with good intentions both for the *Belle*'s black slave cook, Otto, and for himself, a virgin and a blunderer in search of a wife.

The Stories of Eva Luna Isabelle Allende

'Vibrant and colourful . . . twenty-three magical tales, of anger that changes to laughter and revenge that turns into love' – *Literary Review*. 'Like a plate of hors-d'oeuvres, each one tempting, some as exquisite as caviare . . . stunning' – *The New York Times Book Review*

Shards of Memory Ruth Prawer Jhabvala

The Master, an enigmatic spiritual leader, has an influence which spreads through four generations and across three continents. Elsa Kopf, a wealthy American, moves from New York to Hampstead to dedicate herself to the dissemination of the Master's message. Deserting her husband, Kavi, an Indian poet, she and her companion Cynthia take up the cause of the great man. 'Jhabvala weaves this dance of generations with economy and humour . . . her gallery of characters is vividly realized' – *The Times*

A CHOICE OF FICTION

No Night is Too Long Barbara Vine

Tim Cornish, a creative-writing student, sits composing a confession: an admission of a crime committed two years ago that has yet to be discovered. 'A dark, watery masterpiece ... suffused with sexuality, which explores with hypnotic effect the psychological path between passion and murder' – *The Times*

Peerless Flats Esther Freud

Lisa has high hopes for her first year in London. She is sixteen and ambitious to become more like her sister Ruby. For Ruby has cropped hair, a past and a rockabilly boyfriend whose father is in prison. 'Freud sounds out as a clear, attractive voice in the literary hubbub' – *Observer*

One of the Family Monica Dickens

At 72 Chepstow Villas lives the Morley family: Leonard, the Assistant Manager of Whiteley's, his gentle wife Gwen, 'new woman' daughter Madge and son Dicky. Into their comfortable Edwardian world comes a sinister threat of murder and a charismatic stranger who will change their lives for ever. 'It is the contrasts that Dickens depicts so rivetingly ... she captures vividly the gradual blurring of social divisions during the last days of the Empire' – *Daily Mail*

Original Sin P. D. James

The literary world is shaken when a murder takes place at the Peverell Press, an old-established publishing house located in a dramatic mock-Venetian palace on the Thames. 'Superbly plotted ... James is interested in the soul, not just in the mind, of a killer' – *Daily Telegraph*

In Cold Domain Anne Fine

'A streamlined, ruthlessly stripped-down psychological family romance with enough plot twists and character revelations to fuel a book three times as long, as wicked and funny as anything Fay Weldon has written. Anne Fine is brilliant' – *Time Out*